THEY AIMED TO DELIVER

Also by Charles Jackson

The Arbiter

THEY AIMED TO DELIVER

Charles F. Jackson

Ashokan Books - Cary, North Carolina

Published by Ashokan Books

ISBN 0-9651797-0-2

LCCN 96-84235

Cover design: Charles Jackson

A Naval Armed Guard crew fires their gun, aboard the SS William J. Worth, in September of 1943. Photo courtesy Nimitz Library, U.S. Naval Academy Annapolis, Maryland 21402

Produced by Windsor Associates, San Diego, CA

This story is dedicated to the gallant men of the U.S. Naval Armed Guard and their courageous shipmates of the U.S. Merchant Marine, who, together, carried the necessary supplies of war to our allies and armies overseas.

The book is based on events that occurred during World War II in the Atlantic and Pacific Oceans and the Mediterranean Sea.

FOREWORD

In the first six months after Pearl Harbor and America's entry into World War II, six German U-boats sank half the total registered tonnage of the U.S. Merchant Fleet.

This novel is based on a few of the many events which involved members of the U.S. Naval Armed Guard, an elite group of American sailors which manned the guns of previously unarmed merchant vessels, during the days of WWII.

The Armed Guard, in spite of high casualties, helped the huge convoys of merchant ships to make it safely through a blanket of German submarines in the Atlantic, the fiercely contested Mediterranean, and the risky Pacific and Indian oceans, during the violent days of the war. The Armed Guard, originally set up during WWI, served during WWII on over six thousand ships. Nearly 145,000 sailors made up this collection of "unsung heroes," as they were called by Winston Churchill, England's Prime Minister during WWII.

The Chairman of the Merchant Marine said, at the end of the war, "If it was not for the merchant seaman, the war would have been lost by the allies. And if it were not for the U.S. Navy Armed Guard gun crews and Armed Guard personnel, the ships and men of the maritime would have been lost, and so would the war."

PREFACE

The history of the U.S. Navy Armed Guard of World War II will never be told in its entirety since the crew was not allowed to keep any kind of record, other than the officer in charge, and he was limited. Some of the crew "slipped" and kept a diary, but these were short in nature. The National Archives of the United States in Washington, D.C. has some of the records captured on microfilm. The true picture of what took place aboard ship is not written in but a few books, and most of these in short stories -- the true feeling of being an Armed Guard would have to come from the person himself, for each has his little part in its history to share -- some good, and some not so good.

It would not be fair to mention one single person by name other than to fully describe what actually is historically valuable in a documented letter of fact so that the unknown may be brought to light in describing as much as possible the labor, suffering, hardship, joy and laughter that were a part of an Armed Guard's life from day to day.

144,970 Armed Guard Crew served -- along with many Merchant Mariners, Army and Marines -- and regular Navy -- Air Corps and Coast Guard of the U.S.A., and allies who escorted us to our destinations. They also risked their lives in search and rescue of our comrades for days after their ships had been sunk.

It is with regret that so many acts of bravery and heroism by those who performed them cannot be entered in the records, by name. What really matters is that the Allies were the "Victors" in the outcome, instead of the "Victims."

Charles A. Lloyd, Chairman,
U.S. Naval Armed Guard Veterans of WWII
Raleigh, N.C.

Special Thanks to:

Charles A. Lloyd, Chairman,
U.S. Naval Armed Guard Veterans of WWII
Raleigh, N.C.

Justin F. Gleichauf, author of "Unsung Sailors,"
the history of the U.S. Naval Armed Guard
(copyright 1990, U.S. Naval Institute Press,
Annapolis, Md.)

The men of the Armed Guard Association who
have shared their experiences.

PROLOGUE

-1942-

Kapitanleutnant Hardegren peered through the periscope at the dark silhouette of the tanker, passing Diamond Shoals off North Carolina's Cape Hatteras. It was 1:30 a.m. on the eighteenth of January, just six weeks after the Japanese attack on Pearl Harbor.

Hardegren knew the ship was heavily loaded, by the way it rode, deep in the water. He suspected it was carrying crude oil from some South American port, headed north, toward the American refineries.

The German U-boat commander ordered one torpedo fired at the slowly-moving ship.

The deadly missile struck the old tanker amidships and ripped the vessel open. A huge ball of fire enveloped the vessel and men began pouring out of hatches and portholes, finally managing to free the number 2 lifeboat and get it into the water, with eight men aboard. Panic stricken, the eight managed to clear the flaming hulk and make their way through the burning crude oil.

Screams pierced the pitch-black night as men became human torches, leaping into the fiery furnace of flaming oil. Not one survived.

The ship foundered, broke in two and slowly sank into the hissing hell-like inferno.

Kapitanleutnant Hardegren lowered the periscope and ordered a note made in U-123's log of his first American kill.

CHAPTER 1

-1992-

Whitey Houston could not believe it. The letter began "On behalf of President M. Gorbachev ..." Gorbachev had resigned as President of the USSR just a few weeks before -- on Christmas, if Whitey remembered correctly.

He continued reading the letter. "... outstanding courage and personal contribution to the allied support of the people of the Soviet Union who fought for freedom against Nazi Germany." It went on to say that the medal accompanying the letter (an elegant thing, thought Whitey) had been struck in honor of the "40th Anniversary of the Victory in the Great Patriotic War."

Whitey would need to think about this awhile. The idea just would not seem to sink in. He'd gotten a telephone call from the U.S. Navy Armed Guard Association just last week, telling him that he, along with over 100 other sailors and veterans of World War II were eligible for the medal, but never thought he'd ever hear anything further.

Whitey was sixty-seven, and still had all his hair and most of his teeth, a bit unusual for people of his generation. He was a short man, and a few pounds overweight these days, but that was the norm. He had looked at the world through a pair of earnest blue eyes all his life, and people who had dealings with him seemed to sense that he could be trusted. Everyone always knew where they stood with Whitey, and possibly that was one of his weak points. Diplomacy was not his strongest suit.

He may have been on the down side of sixty, but he remembered those WWII days as vividly, if not more so, than events of last week - the almost-suicidal convoys to Murmansk, carrying gasoline, ammunition, tanks, and the tools of war, with the Germans incessantly attacking, the air assaults by swarms of German bombers and torpedo planes, and the onslaughts of the submarine Wolf Packs. Sailors said that two of every three ships in the Murmansk runs never came back.

1

The Pacific war, however, was entirely another matter. Whitey could think of his former German enemy now in gentler terms, but the Japanese would forever be among his least favorite people. Yes, he realized that the Japanese he'd fought against in the Pacific were, for the most part, gone now. And their leaders had either died or been executed. The Japanese people of 1992 were a different breed -- everyone said that. Nevertheless, there was no love for the Japanese left in him. The best thought he could muster was tolerance -- no more than this.

He thought of all his former shipmates, many of whom were dead, and of those still living, now in their late sixties, some in their seventies. He would always remember them as they were in those days, young, full of energy, ready to meet and defeat the enemy, brimming with patriotism. Those who made it through the conflict had changed, though. Their energy had been expended, their hate for the enemy, in most cases, was gone. And the patriotism -- perhaps only the older Americans knew and appreciated that idea.

His mind wandered back fifty years in time.

CHAPTER 2

Chief Petty Officer Tressler sat back in his chair and looked at the tall young civilian sitting across the desk from him. The man was older than the average person trying to enlist in the Navy -- 29, according to the papers in front of the chief. He looked to be in good health, and was, according to the physical examination clipped to his papers. Good health, that is, except for the punctured eardrum. The chief suspected that it had something to do with his job as a police officer for the town of Catskill. Maybe someone had fired a pistol next to his ear. Or an explosion. Either one of them could have done it.

The chief had been assigned here only a month, but knew of Jack Houston. Houston, although thin and balding, and looking very much like everyone's image of a wimp, was well thought of in town. Catskill's Chief of Police considered him one of his best officers, and one of the toughest. But Chief Tressler, a heavy-set man in his early fifties, and a 30-year veteran of the Navy, was more impressed with Houston's wife, Loretta. God, the woman was pretty. If it wasn't for her acid tongue and nasty temper she would be a real doll -- just over five feet tall, blue-eyed and blond. But the chief's mind told him to get back to the unpleasant business at hand.

"Your physical looks real good," said Tressler. "but the doc says you've got a punctured ear drum. And he says we've got to turn you down. I'm sorry as hell about this, Jack. The Navy could really use a mature man like yourself, especially with the krauts and japs looking like they're about to give us some real headaches."

Jack had known about the ear drum, but hoped he could get by with it. The chief was right about the Japanese and the Germans. The whole situation spelled trouble, as far as Jack was concerned, and his mind had been set on getting into the service before a war started. He hadn't felt as strongly about anything in his life and the news was a bad blow.

"Chief, isn't there anything you can do? Hell, a punctured ear drum is nothing. I'm in good shape and my training would make me a real asset to the Navy. I want to do something for the country. If things get really bad, they'd probably eventually draft me anyway."

"Jack," said the chief sympathetically, "I can't do a damn thing unless the Navy changes its requirements. You know I'd try to help -- we need good people, and I know you're a good man. Hell, everyone in Catskill knows that, but the Navy regs say that we can't take you."

Tressler could easily tell that Houston was deeply disappointed. Houston's dark eyes averted the chief's gaze, and the man's face mirrored his disappointment.

The chief appeared to be thinking. He hesitated for a moment, then said, "Jack, let me toss an idea at you. If you really want to get into things, have you thought about the Merchant Marine? They're going to be involved right up to their eyebrows, if we get sucked into a war. Right now they're pushing hard to get good people. And the ear drum wouldn't keep you out. Shit, my uncle is sixty-five years old and blind in one eye, and he's a second mate on a tanker that works the Gulf of Mexico. The money is a hell of a lot more than we could pay you in the Navy. If you're interested, I could have the papers sent up from New York City. You might want to go down there and talk to them."

He was a little surprised at the chief's suggestion. Why hadn't he given that some thought? There wasn't much difference between the Navy and the Merchant Marine, as far as he knew. And the chief was right – the money would be better there. His mind began chewing on this very interesting development.

Jack got up from his chair, and shook hands with the other man. As he turned to leave the office, he stopped, hesitated, and then turned back to Tressler.

"Chief Tressler, thanks for all your trouble. This business about the Merchant Marine is something I hadn't thought about. I'll talk it over with Loretta. I'd appreciate it if you would get those papers for me."

"Hell, Jack, no sooner said than done. Give me a couple of days. I'll make a phone call and they'll be on their way."

CHAPTER 3

"**A**re you out of your mind?" shrieked Loretta. "You're twenty-nine years old, with a wife and two children. You've got a good job with the police department -- a promotion coming up. They can't draft you into any of the services. You're safe. You owe it to your family to stay out of this. What's gotten into you?"

Loretta Houston was a small woman, just a fraction over five feet tall. She had a figure that was the envy of the other women in Catskill, and her honey-blonde hair and striking blue eyes made everyone take a second look when she walked past.

Jack and Loretta had been seeing each other for almost a year when she discovered that she was pregnant with Donna, their 10-year-old.

Jack already was a Catskill village police officer, although a rookie, but it was considered a good steady job in those days, and the two wasted no time in getting married.

Loretta's mother, a widow for several years, rented the young couple a bungalow just outside the village. The rent was reasonable and the Houstons were a happy couple, at least for the first few years.

Karen, their youngest daughter, was born two years later, and married life began to change for Jack.

Loretta had always been a quiet girl, but something within her began surfacing -- something that seemed to make her a harder person, more aggressive and unyielding. Jack thought it was a streak of stubbornness and at first laughed it off, but as time went by he found himself yielding to her wishes, rather than risking a painful argument. It was easier to give in to Loretta and avoid the fury of her anger, which was something to behold.

"Loretta," said Jack, "the whole country will be at war, no telling how soon. I can't just stand by and watch everyone else doing their bit. It's true that they wouldn't draft me now, but who knows about later? I wanted to get into the Navy, but they wouldn't take me. It would be the same with the Army. Chief Tressler said the Merchant Marine was looking for people. The pay wouldn't be that good at first, but it would get better -- and I would at least be helping out. I can't explain how strongly I feel about this -- but please, try to understand."

Loretta was upset, and her lips compressed into a tight line.

"Jack, I swear to you -- if you go through with this idiotic idea, I'll leave you, and I'll take Donna and Karen with me. If you think I'm not serious, just try me!"

"I'm going down to New York next week to talk to the Merchant Marine people," said Jack.

At that instant, Loretta realized that Jack had made up his mind. She burst out crying and ran from the room.

CHAPTER 4

The morning crowd was gathered in Aggie's Diner, in the center of the upstate New York town of Catskill. Some sat at the long counter in front of the room, reading their papers and drinking coffee. Others were at booths and tables out back in the big noisy dining room.

The air was filled with the smell of tobacco smoke and frying potatoes, and bacon, eggs and corned beef hash sizzled on the busy grill, with Doug the cook presiding over the activities.

Aggie did not exist, and never did. The restaurant was owned by Teddy Kolokotrones, and it was easy for people to see why he did not name it for himself. Rumor had it that Aggie was Teddy's first love when he came to Catskill from Greece, at the turn of the century. Teddy, short, fat, jolly and well past seventy, wandered around the place, joking, slapping backs and gossiping. He loved to socialize in the mornings.

Ruthie Weiss came by the booth where Floyd Houston and Catskill's Chief of Police George Lamoreaux sat and filled their coffee cups, without asking. Ruthie had been a waitress at the diner since she'd gotten out of high school, ten years ago. She was efficient, but plain as a post and seldom spoke with the customers. She would probably work at Aggie's as long as it remained in business.

Floyd Houston was a locomotive engineer with the New York Central railroad and this was his day off. Tomorrow, he would be doing the Albany to New York run, and the next day he'd be going from Albany to Syracuse, laying over that night, then proceeding to Buffalo early the next morning. He was seldom home more than one or two days at a time and his wife of thirty-five years, Emma, had grown used to his absences. Floyd was a bald-headed bear of a man, well over six feet tall and weighing 250 pounds, but there was no question who ran the Houston household. Emma, a big woman herself, laid down the law for her five boys, and woe betide the one who chose to disobey it.

Emma was a serious and deeply religious woman, and her five children had always attended Sunday school at the local Methodist church.

Always that is, until her son Jack joined the small Catskill police force. His duty often had him working on Sundays and he became a part-time attendee at church services. Emma's pride and joy was her set of twins, Jefferson and Alexander. Neither had ever missed Sunday school nor church, and sang in the choir, where Emma was the director and organist. The strapping dark-haired eighteen-year-olds were nearly identical twins and did not smoke, drink nor gamble.

In sharp contrast to the Houston twins was Whitfield, or Whitey, as he was called locally, probably because of his white-blonde hair. He had recently quit attending church and Sunday School and although he was only sixteen, managed to get his hands on a drink now and then. Whitey had been a smoker for at least three years. He loved to fight and gamble and was just beginning to get interested in women. His twin brothers, Jeff and Lex, were determined to save his soul from hell. Whitey made up in aggressiveness what he lacked in height, and he was sensitive about his lack of stature. Several bigger boys had learned to their sorrow that Whitey could be a tiger, in spite of his size.

Will Houston was the youngest of the boys and the least noticed, both at home and around town. He was a short chunky boy of fifteen, the quiet cherub. But the quietness could be deceiving because he possessed the most violent temper of all the Houstons. Football was his passion and the high school coach was looking forward to Will's moving up to the varsity in 1942.

"Floyd," said the thin and intense Chief Lamoreaux, "you've got to do something about that kid of yours -- Whitey. Phil Harrison had the duty and found him last Saturday night, just after midnight, shit-faced, out behind the hardware store. Someone gave him a bottle of Mogan-David wine and he and Phyllis Haver were having themselves a little party. Phil thought it was pretty funny, but he took Phyllis home -- she caught hell from her mother -- and he brought Whitey over to the station house and sobered him up. He puked all over the office. A hell of a mess. Phil told me and I knew you'd want to hear about it. I didn't want Emma to lower the boom on the kid. She probably knows about it anyway. Mrs. Haver was sure to have called her."

"I don't know how to handle that kid, George. I'm away a lot, and Emma has been trying to rein him in, but he's a stubborn one. I whacked him around some a couple of months ago, but it's done no good at all. I guess it could be worse -- he is managing to get passing grades in school. I asked Jack to talk to him, Jack being a police officer and all, but Jack has his own problems with Loretta, and he's got the two girls, Donna and Karen to worry about. Thanks for letting me know. Maybe it's time for me to take the razor strap to him again."

"What a difference, right in the same family. Take Jack, for instance,

Floyd. He's probably the best officer we have. When I retire in two years, Jack could be in a good position to take my job. I've told Jack that I'm asking the town council to vote him a raise at their next meeting, and believe me, he deserves it."

Floyd Houston smiled with pleasure. He'd always been proud of Jack, but he secretly thought his son was turning into a milquetoast the last couple of years. Loretta had a constant burr under her saddle for some reason, and she treated him poorly. But hell, it hadn't hurt his performance on the police force, and there were few people in town who enjoyed the respect that Jack got from everyone.

Teddy came over to their table and sat down, motioning for Ruthie to bring him a cup of coffee.

"Chief, and Mr. Houston, how you doing? Hey, you see how those damn Nazis invade Greece? We kick out those Italians, you bet, then they have to get Hitler to help them. But you wait -- we kick out Nazis too!"

Neither Chief Lamoreaux nor Floyd gave a damn what the Nazis did to the Greeks. They had their own problems, and hoped that the U.S. wouldn't be pulled into the war, although it looked like it was about to happen. They both thought Roosevelt wanted that.

Teddy rambled on for awhile about the war in Europe, then seemed to sense that no one cared. He laughed, got up, and went behind the counter to check on things there.

"Chief -- I'm obliged to you for letting me know about Whitey. And thanks for not locking him up, although god knows it might do him some good to spend a night in jail. The kid needs something, for sure."

Chief Lamoreaux nodded and Floyd left the diner.

CHAPTER 5

It was November of 1941, and the icy winds from Sheepshead Bay blew across the assembly area of the sprawling United States Maritime Training station in New York City. Jack guessed there were thousands of others standing out in the weather, waiting to be addressed by the commanding officer of the center. Back in Catskill, Chief Tressler had told him that many old-hand merchant marine men were being commissioned as Naval Reserve officers and put in charge of the training centers.

Most of the men standing with Jack were much younger than he -- some only seventeen, but most in their early twenties.

The men were a laughing and amiable group and some of them jokingly called each other "draft-dodger" and "slacker." They had been issued clothing much like that given to the U.S. Navy, a blue uniform with a bright red insignia, without the familiar bell-bottoms, and with pockets. A round blue-dyed watch cap topped off the outfit, and because the weather was cold, the men wore heavy woolen coats, identical to the Navy's pea-coat, but its plain, black buttons did not display the familiar Navy anchor.

A letter from President Franklin D. Roosevelt was read over the public address system, praising them for what they might do for their country in the coming months and years, and suggesting that each one of them possessed qualities that would make them gallant merchant seamen.

Eighteen hundred instructors shivered and stamped their feet as they stood by in the cold while the commanding officer of the station spoke to the men, encouraging them and praising their abilities. They had been standing in formation for nearly two hours, and were thoroughly chilled and ready to go indoors.

Over the twelve-week training period Jack had walked the concrete decks of the training ship "S.S. Dry Land," which had been laid out and built on the grounds of the station. Three short masts had been erected fore and aft of the deckhouse, which stood amidships. The instructors, all experienced merchant mariners, had attempted to teach the green newcomers what they could about shipboard life, including how to take care

11

of themselves while lending a helping hand to their shipmates aboard a vessel at sea.

Jack met a young merchant marine recruit named Stewart Oakley one morning in the mess hall. Stewart had helped his father farm a huge spread in Ames, Iowa. He was 4-F in the draft, due to a heart murmur, probably caused by rheumatic fever when he was ten years old. He was big, blond, noisy and friendly. He'd come to New York City with a dream of seeing the world from the deck of a merchant vessel, and earning what was rumored to be big money.

"Damn, Jack," he said, "I hear those women in Portugal and Spain are hot -- really hot, not like those ice cubes we have back in Iowa. I intend to find out for myself."

It was a very unlikely friendship -- the 29-year-old ex-Catskill police officer, the father of two kids, and a burly ex-corn farmer from Iowa, but the two men somehow hit it off, and went through their training together.

Jack learned the principles of steering by compass, with the help of a "floating" platform, equipped with a ship's wheel and binnacle. He learned what orders to expect when at the helm and how to carry them out, and something of the ship's bridge routine. He and his school shipmates ran winches and rigged cargo gear. They practiced the never-ending routine maintenance work that every ship required. They were taught the best ways to avoid death in the water. Many of them, they were told, might find themselves in flaming oil floating on the surface of the ocean, sometimes without a life jacket. He'd fashioned himself a life-preserver by knotting a pair of trousers and filling them with air by swinging them over his head, as he jumped into the station's swimming pool. The men were warned about poisonous ocean-going snakes. What good would a warning be? The experienced merchant men said the bite of some of those snakes would kill a man in less than a minute. Sharks, barracuda, Portuguese Men-of-War, Sting Rays, all these could cripple or seriously injure a swimmer.

Lookout duty was stressed heavily and the men learned that a lighted cigarette could be clearly seen for nearly a mile. The submarine threat was discussed at length in their classes.

"Men," advised Jack's instructor in their final training class, "you don't know what kind of ship you'll be working on, or what ocean you'll be in. You'll ship out first through the union hall here in New York. Your pay will go up from the fifty bucks you've gotten each month while you were here, to maybe $150 a month, possibly more, depending on the jobs you land. Oh yeah, even though you may dress like swabbies, you don't have to take any shit from the Shore Patrol or the MP's. Good luck to you all!"

CHAPTER 6

Lex pulled over to the curb, where Loretta had been waiting for him. She climbed into his '38 Dodge and smiled. He couldn't help thinking how pretty she was - but he had to be careful of these sinful thoughts. It just wasn't Christian.

As they drove along route 9-W, Loretta moved closer to him. Lex began to feel uncomfortable. This was Jack's wife and she represented the "forbidden fruit." He had no business being alone with her, late at night. But she'd needed a ride back from town and he wasn't doing anything, so it made sense that he could help her out. She'd almost pleaded with him on the telephone. He knew that Loretta could be a shrew at times -- and he'd often wondered how his brother Jack ever put up with her. But she was being real nice now.

"Alex, honey, could you pull into that parking space behind the old burned-out garage just up ahead? I need to look in my purse to see if I still have the receipt for that pair of shoes I bought. I'll be needing it to exchange them when I go back into Catskill. And hand me that flashlight you keep under the seat."

Lex felt a little uncomfortable at this request. She could check her purse just as well when she got home, couldn't she? Why did they have to stop here? Something was fishy. He was suspicious, but at the same time curious and aroused.

He pulled the car around on the concrete behind the garage. The place had gone up in flames early last year, leaving just a front wall of cinder blocks and some steel posts. Some of the local high school kids had begun using the spot for their heavy petting.

Lex parked and set the handbrake. Loretta leaned over him, then reached under his seat for the flashlight he always kept there. As she did, her arm brushed the inside of his right leg, and her breast rested on his thigh. Lex had done a little "fooling around" with his girl friend, Fay, but both of them were very religious, and kept a tight rein on their emotions. This was something new for Lex.

Loretta's perfume was picked up by the air coming from Lex's heater and brought up into his nostrils. His head was beginning to spin -- and then he noticed that Loretta was making no effort to get the flashlight. Her hand closed around his leg, then began to move up toward his crotch.

Lex knew that he should be doing something -- anything -- but in spite of his deeply religious feelings, he felt helpless at this point. It wasn't an unpleasant sensation. To add to his embarrassment, he felt himself getting hard, and knew that Loretta was actively involved in helping him along.

Loretta twisted around in her seat, laying across his lap, then took his left hand and placed it on her breast. Lex was about to protest, or say something, but she reached up with her right arm and pulled his head down -- then kissed him, running her tongue into his mouth as she did so.

He could not remember the sequence of events, or exactly what followed, but knew that Loretta had him by the hand, leading him out of the car, then into the back seat. He was like a zombie, unable to resist -- or was it that he didn't want to resist?

Then they were across the back seat. Loretta had taken off his pants and underwear, and helped him to remove her blouse and bra, then her skirt and panties. Suddenly, he found Loretta astride him, guiding him into herself. With a rush, it was all over for Lex, but Loretta seemed like a crazed animal, bucking and groaning and twisting and turning. Lex seemed to be watching everything outside of himself, much as an observer. Finally, with a long moan, Loretta was finished, and collapsed over Lex.

As Lex and Loretta dressed, he began to feel a sense of guilt overwhelming him. He had given in to the weakness of his body and committed adultery with his brother's wife. He was guilty of breaking one of the ten commandments. Shame began to settle on him.

What happened then puzzled him. They got back into the front seat and he started the car, then headed back out onto the highway. Loretta was humming a tune, and acted as if nothing had taken place. She began talking about how her kids, Donna and Karen, were doing in school. She talked and talked, on and on, but Lex didn't listen. His mind was numb and didn't follow most of what she said. He was confused and ashamed, and said nothing all the way back to Loretta's house, where he dropped her off and said good night.

Lex had learned a painful lesson this night, the first of many that he would absorb in the next few years. The sex act could be one of deepest love and affection, as his idealistic young mind saw it. Or it could be just simply the satisfying of an animal urge, much as eating when hungry, or sleeping when tired. He realized then that Loretta had used him.

CHAPTER 7

-1942-

The Shamrock bar on New York City's 86th street was jammed with men -- merchant seamen, American and British sailors, and a sprinkling of seagoing men from all over the world. The bar was a busy place and the beer and whiskey poured from the bottles like water. Some very attractive young ladies of the evening also plied their trade from table to table and along the bar. Although the world was at war, people still sought escape, some through alcohol, others in the arms of strangers.

On the walls of the place were signs, proclaiming "A slip of the lip -- May sink a ship" and "Don't blab -- the enemy is listening."

"Honey," said the young merchant seaman, "let's you and me go find a nice hotel room and pitch some woo. Two days from now my ship is setting sail for Liverpool and I'll be mighty lonesome for a few weeks."

"Stewart, you know I'm not that kind of a girl. What would my parents think? Buy me another drink and tell me about Liverpool. I've always wanted to see England -- but not now, of course, with the Germans dropping all those terrible fire bombs."

Stewart, a big blond happy-go-lucky kid, and by now half drunk, focussed his eyes on a waiter and motioned for two more drinks. The smiling waiter nodded and headed for the bar to pick them up, noting that the two were both drinking rum cokes.

"Hell, Gracie, we must have 300 jeeps and a lot of tanks aboard my ship. They've been loading for four days, and we've been putting fuel oil and wheat aboard. I guess the limeys can use everything we can get to them."

"When will you be coming back, Stewart?"

"God only knows. Sometimes we have to take a side trip to Africa and pick up cargo to bring back to the States. That old rust bucket I sail on, the SS Provident, was built in 1910. Sure hope we don't hit any hard weather -- it might break apart."

Stewart laughed as he said this. The truth of the matter was that the Provident was a sturdy merchant vessel and had made many transits of the

Atlantic, in stormy weather and calm seas, and was known as a "lucky" ship by all the crews who sailed in her.

The night wore on and Stewart was pretty seriously drunk. Gracie excused herself and left, and it was doubtful if Stewart noticed.

Gracie caught the subway to her apartment in Brooklyn. Instead of going directly to her room, she climbed the stairs to an apartment on the building's top floor and knocked on a door at the end of the hallway.

The door opened and she went directly in.

"Carl," said Gracie, "I've got some information for you. You'd better warm up the transmitter."

Within an hour, Admiral Dönitz' Command Center had the intelligence and the next day Lieutenant Commander Kals in U-130 was assigned his next target.

Three days later, the young U-boat commander sent the S.S. Provident to the bottom of the Atlantic, in a flaming mass of burning oil and screaming men.

CHAPTER 8

George Smiley was just a few bricks short of a full load, maybe even a bit slow, but he managed to handle his job of delivering telegrams for Western Union in Catskill. He was a small man, dark-skinned and dark-eyed, looking much younger than his twenty-five years. He'd been with WU since he was eighteen and loved his job and the responsibilities it gave him.

It was an unusually cold day for January. The sides of the road were covered with snow drifts and the ice lay in patches along the highway. George was bundled up with earmuffs, muffler and heavy gloves. As he rode his bicycle along route 209 just outside of Catskill, on the way to Loretta and Jack Houston's bungalow, he wondered about the black-bordered envelope he carried. Although he hadn't seen one before, he suspected it contained bad news. Unknown to George, he would be delivering many of these in the next few years.

Loretta answered George's knock and turned to ice when she saw him standing there. He smiled and handed her the telegram.

"You've got to sign here, on my delivery sheet, Mrs. Houston," he said.

Loretta, in a daze, signed the sheet and gave George a quarter. The young man swung aboard his bicycle and headed back toward Catskill, along the blacktop highway, whistling as he pedalled along.

Loretta was filled with fear and foreboding. She had never received a telegram in her life, but knew that they usually carried bad news. She tore the envelope open and read the terse words:

"Regret to inform you that your husband, John R. Houston, is missing at sea and presumed to be lost."

It was signed "Howard E. Brown, Standard Oil of New Jersey."

She collapsed by the door.

CHAPTER 9

The Catskill Mountain News carried the story a few days later. The Esso Tanker S.S. Alan Jackson had been sunk early in the morning of the eighteenth of January. Only eight men of its 50-man crew had survived, and Catskill's own Jack Houston was one of the missing. Although the Navy had tried to keep the news from the papers, they had not succeeded, since this was the first American tanker sunk since the war had begun in December of the previous year. It was rumored that two more tankers had also been attacked, presumably by German submarines, along the east coast.

Floyd and Emma Houston were desolate and in deep despair. Loretta and her children were being attended to by her mother at home.

People have different ways of facing tragedy. Some refuse to accept that anything has happened and continue their lives as if that were true. Others suffer deep psychological damage and never do recover. Some become hysterical for a time, then slowly recuperate and eventually resume their normal lives.

The Houston twins, Jeff and Lex, belonged to the last group. They leaned heavily on their religious upbringing, receiving support from their girl friends and their pastor. Lex believed he was being punished by God for his brief romantic fling with Jack's wife, just a few weeks before. He had not spoken to Loretta since, and she had made no attempt to talk to him.

No one in town knew or suspected that Jack's death had struck Whitey harder than any of the Houston family. He tried not to show it. Whitey thought of himself as a very tough young man. A public show of sorrow would tell the world that he was a softy, and that would not do. Although he did not realize it, Whitey would carry a deep mental scar for the rest of his life. Jack had been his hero, someone he could imitate, and now he was gone. Someone must pay.

Will, the youngest Houston boy, tried to erase Jack's death from his mind. When he thought of Jack, which was often, he told himself that somehow Jack had survived. Maybe he was on some island off the coast of North Carolina. Without a funeral, a coffin and a burial service, Will could not accept the death of his brother. The Methodist Church had held a memorial service on the weekend following the announcement of the ship's sinking, and the town's citizens turned out in great numbers. Jack had been a popular police officer and a well-liked man, and his memory began to assume heroic stature, deserved or not.

A plaque was placed near the flagpole on the town square, in memory of Jack, and a brief ceremony was conducted. In twenty years it would disappear, and no one would bother to replace it.

CHAPTER 10

The 1935 Ford roadster lay on its side in a ditch along New York's route 9W. Marks on the blacktop highway showed that the car had hit a patch of ice, spun wildly several times and gone into the ditch. A wrecker would be needed to pull the vehicle out.

Trooper Reed had the car's drunken and dazed occupant in the back of his patrol car. He pulled back onto the highway, heading for Catskill.

Back at the police station the trooper and Chief Lamoreaux were talking.

"Damn, Chief Lamoreaux, this kid is sloshed to the gills. Maybe that's why he doesn't seem to be hurt. Hell, he isn't even bleeding, but the car he was driving is a mess. His license says he's Whitfield Houston. Isn't that John's brother?"

"I knew this was going to happen, sooner or later, Sergeant Reed. If you don't mind, I'll take care of this -- that should save you some paperwork, and I'd appreciate it."

"Suits me, Chief. It's nearly midnight and almost the end of my shift. I'll drop over to the all-night diner and get me some breakfast, then go on home."

"Thanks, Sarge. I'll see that Art Wilson gets out there first thing in the morning and pulls the car out of the ditch. I owe you a favor."

Mrs. Houston answered the telephone. She knew that it would be bad news, coming at this time of night.

"Mrs. Houston, Whitey's had an accident with his car, just outside of town. A State Trooper brought him in here, and I've got him in a cell. He's not hurt, but he's had too much to drink, and I need to keep him overnight. Just wanted you to know. I'd like to talk to you in the morning. I think it's about time that we straightened Whitey out, somehow or other."

"Oh my god, Chief," said Mrs. Houston. "He promised he'd stop that booze, and quit smoking, and I believed him. I've tried to raise him properly, but he's just too wild for me. I wish Floyd was here, but he's spending the night down in Kingston and won't be back until tomorrow afternoon. Could we come down to the jail then? Let Whitey stay in a cell at the jail -- maybe it will impress him with the trouble he's gotten himself into. Oh, Lord."

"That's fine with me, Mrs. Houston. I don't plan on charging him with anything, although I could get him for drunken driving. Since no one has been hurt, and this is the first time, we can go easy on him -- but let's not let him know that."

"Thanks, Chief Lamoreaux," said Mrs. Houston. "You've been a good friend to our family."

Chief Lamoreaux, Floyd Houston, Mrs. Houston and Whitey sat at a table in the Catskill police station, the afternoon following Whitey's automobile accident.

Whitey had a headache and the light in the room seemed much too strong for his eyes. In spite of a bowl of soup and a cup of coffee served by Phil Harrison, who had jail duty that day, Whitey's stomach felt on the edge of being sick.

"Son," said Chief Lamoreaux, "we could charge you with drunk driving. In fact, that's what we should do. You're only seventeen, and you've only been driving a year -- we could take your license away for awhile. You could be sent to the reform school up in Elmira. If I could find out who gave you the booze, I'd make some trouble for them too. That's the sum of it. You're in trouble this time, and we've got to figure out how we're going to handle it."

"Whitey," said Will Houston, "that last beating I gave you didn't teach you a lesson at all. I can see that. We've all been too easy on you, and you take advantage of our good natures. Everyone has been trying to help you, and what do we get in return? You smash up the car I helped you buy and make your family look like trash. If you don't care about your own reputation, think about your mother. She hasn't raised you to act like this."

"Whitey, Whitey," sobbed Mrs. Houston. "What are we going to do?"

Whitey knew he'd gotten himself in too deep this time, but he couldn't think of anything to say. He just shook his head. His mother's crying bothered him deeply. He felt like a worthless bum. After his brother Jack's death in January, Whitey had been drinking a lot more than usual, but it didn't do any good. He'd wake up in the morning, feeling depressed and sick. He knew his mother had taken Jack's passing harder than he. There had been no body to bury -- just a memorial service.

Chief Lamoreaux drew his chair up close to the table. His thin fingers held a pencil, which he continually tapped against the table top.

"Here's what I propose, folks. If the county prosecutor heard about this, I'd be forced to bring some charges against Whitey, and even though this is his first offense, he still might end up in Elmira for eight or ten months. That's what happened to the O'Herlihy boy down in Saugerties last month, except when he ran off the road, he had his girl friend with him, and she got banged up pretty bad. Her parents insisted on charges being brought, and the judge down there threw the book at him. We've got a little different situation here."

"Chief," said Whitey, "I promise this won't happen again. Me and a couple of friends just had too much to drink and I hit a patch of ice. I really wasn't that drunk."

"Shut up, Whitey," growled the chief. "Now -- here's the deal. With the war on now, you're due to come up for the draft next year. They're putting most of the young men in the army. If your parents are willing to sign the papers, you can get in any service that you want. Maybe one of the armed forces can pound some sense into that thick skull of yours, I don't know. But that's what I'm offering you -- a chance to get off the hook. If you decide not to take it -- well, you may have to do some jail time. We just can't have our young folks driving drunk. And I don't care if your brother Jack was one of my best friends, and your family means a lot to me. Take it or leave it."

"No," groaned Mrs. Houston, "I don't want to lose another boy. One was far too much. I'll never sign any papers, Chief. A lot of our boys are going to die in this war, I know. I don't want Whitey to be one of them, in spite of the trouble he's in right now."

"Emma, we'll talk about this at home," said Will Houston. "I think the Chief is being fair about the whole thing."

"Talk about it," said the chief. "Before the week is out, let me know what you decide. In the meantime, I'm turning your boy loose, but remember -- I may be forced to bring charges against him, and there's plenty of time for me to do that. Once I get the ball rolling, it's in the hands of the county prosecutor, and he may not be so friendly. And Whitey -- you better give this some thought too. I think you'll realize what I'm offering is for your own good, although you may not think so right now."

Whitey kept his mouth shut. He felt he was looking at some sort of sentence, one way or another, and it looked like he had little choice in the matter.

CHAPTER 11

It was a week after Chief Lamoreaux' ultimatum. Whitey's parents had signed the papers, over his mother's protests, but her husband pointed out that Whitey might be going to prison and that prospect was a worse one than entering the service.

Whitey went to the Navy recruiting office in Catskill's Post Office Building and entered Chief Tressler's office.

"Whitfield Houston, am I right?" asked Chief Tressler.

"Yes, sir," replied Whitey.

"Never mind that sir business, kid, I'm a Chief Petty Officer. You only 'sir' officers. Say, aren't you Jack Houston's kid brother? I was sorry to hear about that. In a way, I feel responsible -- but he knew what he was doing. Chief Lamoreaux called me yesterday and told me you'd be coming in. Okay -- fill out these papers. If everything checks out okay, I'll square things with New York and you'll be on a bus to the Armed Forces Recruiting center down there tomorrow morning. We've got a bunch of you fellows to send. Take only a razor and your toothbrush -- maybe a change of underwear. Your physical should take part of the day and then they'll tell you where you'll be doing your boot camp. It could be anywhere -- at Sampson here in New York State, Great Lakes in Illinois, or maybe in the new center they've just opened in Bainbridge, Maryland."

"Yes, sir," said Whitey.

Chief Tressler handed him a sheaf of papers and a pencil.

"Take these outside. There're a table and chair in the room out there. Fill out everything as best as you know how, then bring the papers back to me. I've already got your parents' approval, since you're only seventeen. If you have any questions, ask me. When you're through, let me check everything out, then you can go back home. Be back here at the office tomorrow morning at seven. There'll be a lot of others waiting here. Eat some breakfast at home -- it's a good ride down to New York City, and you won't be stopping off anywhere. Got all that?"

Whitey nodded and left to do his paperwork.

It was snowing early the next morning and the temperature had dipped to ten degrees. Whitey said goodbye to his parents and left for the Post Office Building. His mother watched him leave from the front room, tears running down her cheeks. Whitey's father, on the other hand, looked proudly at his son, going off to war.

A large group of young men, mostly in their late teens, milled around inside the Post Office and Whitey looked to see if there was anyone in the crowd that he knew. There was not.

As they waited, an old bus pulled to the curb in front of the building. A young petty officer, clipboard in his hand, jumped off the bus. The teen-aged recruits looked him over. He wore a peacoat and what the Navy called a "flat hat," similar to the one worn by the little boy on the familiar Cracker Jack box. His shoes were shined to a spit-polish and his pants displayed the well-known bell-bottoms.

"Okay, men," said the petty officer. "I'll call out your names from my list. As I do, answer `present' and get aboard the bus - and make it snappy, We've got a long way to go and plenty to do when we get to New York City."

With this, the sailor began reading off the names.

Several of the people were not present. Whitey guessed that they'd lost their nerve and decided to back out. He had only contempt for anyone who would do this and could not picture himself backing down on anything, once he'd given his word.

The bus, once loaded, closed its doors and proceeded out of Catskill, along route 9-W and south toward the city.

CHAPTER 12

Whitey was trying to get some sleep on the bus, headed for Bainbridge, Maryland. Everything had happened too fast for him to comprehend. He thought about the events of the day.

There were literally hundreds of men at the Recruiting Center in New York City, undergoing physicals. The examinations were administered by soldiers and sailors, and a battery of doctors directed the activity.

The men were weighed and measured, lined up and checked for hernias, examined again and again. Eyes, ears, throats. Knees were tapped with rubber hammers. Reflexes and stability were noted. Everything seemed to take forever. Lines formed at the various examination stations, dwindled down, then formed again somewhere else. At noon, the men were herded into a nearby cafeteria and fed a hot meal, then herded back to the examination center for more tests.

For Whitey, the physical ended early in the afternoon and he and several dozen others were sent to a large room with a podium, then told to wait. He knew that some of the other recruits were draftees, others enlisting, and that they would be entering the Army, the Marines and the Navy, possibly the Coast Guard.

After an hour of waiting, a petty officer and the first commissioned officer that Whitey had seen, entered the room. The petty officer introduced the officer as Lieutenant Wagner. Wagner went to the podium.

"I am now about to swear you men into the United States Navy. All of you have enlisted, of your own free will. Before I ask you to raise your right hands and take the oath, I must tell you -- if there is anyone who does not wish to be sworn in at this time, now is the time to leave."

Lieutenant Wagner looked around the room. The men glanced at each other. One young man raised his hand. The petty officer went over to him and the two spoke quietly, then both left the room.

Although every man there now felt superior to the unfortunate youth who had decided to leave, even considered him with contempt, all would be envying him in the next week, thinking that they too should have decided to leave.

"Raise your right hands," said Lieutenant Wagner, "and repeat after me."

The men repeated the oath, after Lieutenant Wagner, and were sworn into the Navy. Whitey knew that this was a significant moment for him, and he felt very proud.

Lieutenant Wagner left the room and the petty officer took charge.

"Listen up," he said. "Some of you will be going to San Diego or Great Lakes for training, some to Sampson, and the rest to Bainbridge. Those who are slated for Bainbridge and Sampson will be leaving late today, by bus. Everyone else will be quartered here in New York for the night, and put on trains tomorrow. Stay where you are for now. We'll be taking groups out, one at a time, for the evening meal. When your name is called, go to the corner of the room where the petty officer with the list is standing. You'll stay with that group."

He had fallen asleep, but was awakened as the air brakes of the bus hissed. The vehicle had stopped outside of a gate. A large sign over the sentry building stated *U.S. Naval Training Center, Bainbridge, Md.,* and a young sailor stood outside the bus, checking the papers offered him by the driver. He motioned the bus through the gate.

The bus drove through the large base, with its many gray wooden buildings, finally stopping in front of a brilliantly lit two-story building. Six petty officers directed the men into the building. Over the front door of the structure was a sign, proclaiming 'Welcome Into The Navy'.

Whitey was exhausted and his head was beginning to pound. He felt as if he were recovering from a hangover, but followed the others into a large auditorium. A CPO stood on a stage and when the men were seated in folding chairs, directed them to fill out forms which were distributed to them by petty officers. Whitey struggled through the instructions. Somewhere around two in the morning, the men were again herded out of the building, separated into groups of sixty men each and "marched" to barracks. No one was in step. Some laughed, but were silenced immediately by the petty officers, who seemed stern and unforgiving.

"Grab yourselves a bunk," ordered a CPO, who seemed to be in charge of things. "Don't worry about pillowcases or sheets. There are blankets so you won't freeze your asses off. Reveille will be at 4:30 this morning, so you won't get a hell of a long time to sleep. You can shave and shower then -- there's a towel on every bunk. Sweet dreams."

Whitey climbed into a top bunk. The beds were stacked two-high.

Some of the men laughed and joked, but were soon silenced by the others and it was not long before the entire room was filled with the snores of exhausted would-be sailors.

CHAPTER 13

The racket was ear-splitting. Two petty officers banged the wooden handles of brooms against the sides of garbage cans as the lights snapped on in Whitey's barracks.

"Drop your cocks and grab your socks!" roared the Chief Petty Officer. "You got fifteen minutes to get shaved and showered. Then form up outside. You'll march to chow. Get your asses in gear!"

The petty officers shook some men who had not moved from their bunks, and pushed others out onto the floor. They walked down the rows of double-tiered racks, rattling the wooden broom handles on the iron pipes of the beds, shouting and shaking the frames. Men cursed and complained, but they rolled out of their bunks, grabbed the towels that were on each rack, and hurried to the big bathrooms, known as "heads" in the Navy. Well within the fifteen minutes allotted, the men were assembled in ragged rows outside the barracks, still dressed in their dirty and wrinkled civilian clothes.

The CPO roared again, "Form ranks, four across, and let's see if you shitheads can make it to the chow hall."

The petty officers shoved, pushed, threatened and motioned the men and they finally got moving along the black top road leading from their barracks, to the cavernous chow hall. Hundreds of other recruits also marched in front and behind Whitey's group.

Once they reached the huge and noisy building, the odor of cooking food and the noise of clanking metal trays came from the doors of the place.

The men were lined up in single-file and proceeded into the hall, past metal racks containing food trays, massive coffee cups, knives, forks and spoons. Eventually the line found its way to a series of steam tables, where each recruit was served creamed chipped beef on toast, fried potatoes, and oatmeal. The servers were themselves recruits, but further along in the training process than the raw recruits now passing through the line.

As the men ate, petty officers wearing badges identifying them as Boatswains' Mates walked from table to table, urging the men to "eat everything that's on your tray -- don't throw anything away. When you go

31

through the chow line, take what you want, but eat what you take. You don't leave the chow hall if your tray isn't empty. Hurry up, hurry up, you ain't got all day."

As one group of men would leave the chow hall, another would come in, pass through the steam table line, be seated at the long wooden mess tables, eat, then carry their trays to the window of the scullery, where they would scrape what little was left into garbage cans, then pass the tray, cups and eating utensils to the men working behind the scullery tables. These scullery people themselves were boots, and every man now eating would some day do his one-week duty in the kitchen and behind the steam tables.

Whitey's bunch formed up outside of the chow hall and were quickly marched back to their barracks.

"Stand by, men," said the CPO. "You've got a busy day ahead of you. Take a shit, use the head, but be ready to move out when you're told."

———————————

Hundreds of recruits were lined up in orderly rows in the large assembly area of the supply building and a jumbo cardboard box was placed at the feet of each man.

"Now hear this, men," shouted a supply chief, "Strip down. Everything off and into the boxes -- and I mean everything. I want to see bare asses -- and quick!"

In a matter of moments, hundreds of naked young men stood at attention.

"Now hear this, men,'" shouted the chief again, "take the pencils on the floor and fill out the labels on the boxes with your home address, if you can remember them. All your stuff will be mailed to your hometown, courtesy of Uncle Sam. And get a move on -- we've got to get you skinheads suited up."

Once this was done, the men were marched, single-file, through the supply corridors. At each stop they were measured by petty officers and given clothing -- first shoes and socks, then the regulation navy boxer shorts, known as skivvies.

The new sailors emerged from the supply building with a fresh set of dungarees, consisting of blue chambray shirt, black web belt with brass buckle, and jeans. Each man carried a seabag, a green duffel bag made of heavy canvas, stuffed with all the other articles of clothing. Somewhere during their travels, they'd found the time to stencil their names on nearly every item they received. The Navy did not forget anything, down to tooth paste, shaving gear and comb.

The uniforms all seemed too large, but would eventually fit the men like they were tailor-made. The Navy was in the business of turning boys into men.

They were now ready to begin the next phase of their transformation from green landlubbers to salty sea dogs.

The next few days were frenzied. Each man received a "skinhead" haircut, went through a never-ending series of lines and received medical and psychological examinations, immunizations and "shots," bedding and towels. Each man would undergo a written test to determine his mental acuity and the results of that test would follow each one through his entire naval career.

The period of training for Navy recruits in those days was twelve weeks, and it started off quickly, but as Whitey and his company went through their classroom and field training, time began to move ever more swiftly, and the pace became frantic.

The Naval recruits learned to fight fires aboard ship. The objective of the training was to remove the fear of fire and instill in the men confidence that they could extinguish a fire, using the equipment that the Navy gave them. Every man experienced the thrill of jumping off a 35-foot tower into the swimming pool, which simulated leaping into the water from the deck of a ship, then swimming to the far end and climbing out. Those who could not were given remedial swimming lessons in the evenings, after the day's training was concluded for the others.

The CPO in charge of Whitey's company of boots told the men early one morning "Recruit training can be compared to a compass -- it's an instrument of direction. The Compass Rose of intensive training we're giving you is designed to convert you from landlubber civilians into good sailors, and help you get a leg up in learning about naval life. Listen good, men. What you learn here could save your life later on."

Whitey was surprised to find that even though he was learning to be a bluejacket, he was expected to master military drill and the manual of arms, along with a full understanding of semaphore flags. He and his buddies carried their old Springfield rifles everywhere they marched, and they marched everywhere. The weapons probably hadn't been fired for years, and what little shooting Whitey and the other recruits did was with .22 caliber rifles, on the firing range. He was a little surprised when he posted his boot company's best firing score.

After six weeks, the CPO announced that the men would be allowed their first "liberty" the following Saturday, and could catch busses into Baltimore.

"Jesus, Whitey," said his buddy Marq LeVesque, the young French-Canadian recruit from Maine, "it'll be a blast to get off this shit-faced base and tie into some cold beer. Maybe even find us some sweet young femmes."

"They tell me you have to be twenty-one to get any booze. How're we gonna manage that, LeVesque?"

"Whitey, mon ami, a guy who was there last week said there's a place down on Calvert street. An Italian restaurant and they have a big back room. You can get spaghetti and ravioli and wine, and all the beer you can drink -- so long as you have the cash -- and we've got that, for sure. And he told me about a burlesque house on Baltimore street -- they've got some knockout girls. Hell, we can walk from there to the spaghetti house, drunk or sober."

Whitey could see that this military routine wasn't going to be all spit and polish, after all.

The band played accompaniment as the heavy-set woman went through her strip routine, throwing items of clothing down into the cheering audience. There would be a drum roll, then a thump of the big drum, and another stocking or scarf would fly across the stage. She was not very pretty, nor even very sexy, but she was an artist, and the crowd of sailors applauded that. To be truthful, any woman talented enough to entertain them at this point in their young lives would be well savored.

Every two or three strip routines was followed by a pair of baggy-pants comics, who leered and smirked their way through a series of sight gags and off-color jokes, accompanied by the band drummer's rim shots on his snare drums.

The crowd ate it up and screamed for more. Whitey and LeVesque were caught up in the excitement and novelty of the whole thing. Then, the band struck up a sizzling jazz number and the spotlight swung to the left side of the stage and hesitated momentarily. From out of the curtains came one of the most beautiful young girls that Whitey had ever seen, her flame-red hair accentuated by the brilliant light, and he knew right then that he was in love.

She may not have possessed the artistry of the earlier stripper, but was much younger and infinitely more attractive. As she minced and strutted through her routine, several of the sailors in the front row left their seats and started for the stage, but were met by four husky bouncers who were stationed there for just that eventuality. Though half drunk, the sailors had the sense to know when they should retreat, and they returned to their seats, shouting and clapping as they did so.

The show lasted two hours and when the curtains fell a cheer went up from the assembled spectators, who then made a mad dash for the exits.

"Come on, Whitey," said LeVesque, who was with Mastromarino and

Gallagher, two other sailors from his boot company. "We're headed for Valentino's Spaghetti House. Mastromarino knows how to get there -- he's from Baltimore. The damn place ain't that far."

The banquet room in Valentino's was bursting with sailors. Platters of spaghetti and meat balls were delivered by the waiters and every table had two or three pitchers of beer and bottles of red wine. Most of those there were already drunk and one or two seemed to be either sleeping or passed out in their chairs. Hardly a sailor in the room was older than nineteen.

Whitey and his three buddies took an empty table and ordered spaghetti. Even before their order arrived, they had finished most of the pitcher of beer the waiter had set in front of them, and were clamoring for more.

A juke box in the corner of the room was turned up full, blasting out boogie woogie, Tommy Dorsey and Bing Crosby, and all was right with the world.

Whitey was bursting with pride as his company passed the reviewing stand for Final Review. They had weathered all the challenges that the Recruit Training Command could throw their way, and been christened sailors. Now all that awaited him was to find out where he'd be sent. Could it be one of those powerful battleships, or a majestic aircraft carrier? Possibly a submarine, although Whitey didn't relish that idea. In any case, he'd find out tomorrow, when orders were to be posted. He wondered about his two brothers, Jeff and Lex, who had both enlisted in the Navy in December. His mother had written him that they were to take their training at Geneva, in upper New York State. They'd probably be freezing their asses off, he thought.

Camp Shelton? Where the hell was that? Somewhere in Virginia, a yeoman had said, near Little Creek, wherever that was. Sounded like some damned Army camp. But the training was intended to turn the men into what the Navy called its "Armed Guard." The Chief told Whitey and LeVesque, who had both been chosen for the duty, that they were to be members of an elite crew, something that was, for now, hush-hush.

CHAPTER 14

The bus was loaded to capacity with sailors newly graduated from boot camp, some from Bainbridge, others from Sampson. What the men had in common was that they were to undergo six weeks of training to become members of the Navy's newly-organized Armed Guard.

The Armed Guard had originally been put together in World War I, the "Great War," to combat the awesome successes of the then-new weapon of war, the submarine. Winston Churchill later said, "In April 1917, the great approach route to the southwest of Ireland was becoming a veritable cemetery of British shipping." One of every four ships that left Great Britain never returned.

When Germany notified the U.S. in January of 1917 that any merchant vessel entering its declared war zones would be sunk on sight, President Wilson asked Congress for authority to arm merchants. Congress turned him down, but he proceeded to do it anyway, and it was not long before American merchant vessels were engaging in armed combat with German submarines, managing to sink, damage and fight off many of them. The AG made a good name for itself in that war, and the U.S. Navy and President Roosevelt had not forgotten.

What Whitey and the rest of the men saw from the windows of the bus was a hodge-podge of small buildings, set into what appeared to be a swamp. The bus stopped in front of a one-story barracks, and the men were ordered to assemble inside.

Pot-bellied stoves heated the wooden building, and the cold January winds whistled through the cracks of the place.

Chief Gunner's Mate Harry VanBenschoten and a swarthy little first-class gunner's mate named Silverio stood inside, waiting for their new charges.

"Sound off, men, as I call your names," said Silverio, and he proceeded to read down a muster-list fastened to a clipboard. Two men on the 60-name list were missing.

"Chief VanBenschoten here will now say a few words," said Silverio, and he relinquished his position to the tall and thin Chief.

Every man in the room noted the six gold stripes on the Chief's left sleeve, denoting at least twenty-four years of honorable Naval service, and each was suitably impressed.

Chief VanBenschoten presented a grim appearance, although he was a man of good humor. His weathered face and cold blue eyes probably contributed to that perception, and he was not a man who smiled often during the performance of his Naval duties.

"Six weeks," said the Chief. "That's what the Navy has given me to train you young shitheads. You're going to learn how to identify jap and kraut airplanes and ships -- and that includes their damn subs as well. And you're going to learn how to load and shoot. You'll stand fire watches while you're resting, and you'll learn how to cut kindling wood for the stoves around the Camp. You'll keep those damn things red-hot, or freeze your tender little asses off. Don't worry about liberty for any of those six weeks -- there's no place around here for you to go anyhow. My friend Gunner's Mate Silverio here will be posting a duty roster on the quarterdeck, and we'll begin your training first thing Monday morning. The main reason each one of you is here is that you're in good health. There ain't no doctors aboard the merchant ships you'll be serving on. And they tell me you have 20-20 vision, and can see pretty good at night. Let's hope so."

The Chief turned and left the barracks.

The following week the men were split into crews of five for practice in firing a Mark IX 4-inch gun, which had been used on destroyers in World War I. The guns were located behind the barracks, and at first all training consisted of "dry runs" using dummy ammunition but with no actual firing. Some of the men were put on 3-man crews and trained in the firing of .30 and .50 caliber machine guns.

The men attended classes in the only structure that had classrooms, next to the administration building. The beginning training concentrated d on breaking down and putting together small weapons -- pistols, rifles and machine guns. After a week, they were told they would soon be actually firing, from the deck of a ship.

Finally, the men got the opportunity to fire real ammunition from training ships, the old U.S.S. Dubuque and the equally ancient U.S.S. Paducah, World War I vintage cruisers. The novice gunners shot at a sunken derelict in the Chesapeake Bay. Later, they were bussed to nearby Dam Neck, Virginia, and were able to do their target-practice on objects known as "sleeves" and towed by planes. They blasted away at targets that were floating, pulled slowly behind Navy tugboats.

Whitey got some good advice, which he never forgot, from Silverio.

"Houston, get yourself a good sharp knife and carry it aboard those merchant ships. It's a good idea to have a water-tight flashlight somewhere you can find it -- if you ever get torpedoed, the first things to go are the lights -- and maybe some rope, in case you find yourself overboard and need to tie onto something. And always have a set of clothing handy, heavy stuff if you're in the North Atlantic. It gets colder than a well-digger's ass out there, believe me. Those merchant sailors go schooner-rigged. You know what that means? You store everything that's valuable in a locker before you ship out, and take only what you need aboard ship. It's not a bad idea."

The six weeks flew by. Everyone would have liked to sample some liberty in Norfolk, even though it had a reputation for a town that didn't care much for sailors, to which it owed most of its livelihood, but the training took place at a feverish pitch. The jobs of staying warm, keeping the stoves around Camp Shelton stocked with wood and the ashes cleaned out, along with fire watches and the regularly-scheduled classes and gun drills filled each man's days and part of his nights. The food served in the chow hall was a cut above what they were used to in boot camp, probably because there were less mouths to feed and the cooks could be more creative.

One Thursday evening in February, the men were told that a special meeting would be held the next morning, immediately following morning chow.

The men formed up outside the barracks, with their pea coat collars turned up. That Friday morning, it was sleeting. A cold wind blew in from the Chesapeake Bay. They stamped their feet to keep the circulation going. Whitey guessed the temperature was in the low thirties.

Commander Williford, the camp C.O., arrived in a jeep, with Chief VanBenschoten driving. GM1 Silverio had already formed the sailors in ranks and completed the morning muster.

"Attention on deck," barked Silverio.

"At ease, men," said Commander Williford, the youthful-looking C.O. He was Hollywood's idea of a naval officer, dashing, good-looking and tall. He wore an unbuttoned heavy winter overcoat over his dress-blue uniform, which was impeccable, and two rows of service ribbons could be seen across his left breast. In his hand he carried a sheaf of papers, and Whitey was afraid they were in for some sort of patriotic speech. He was wrong.

"Congratulations on completing your training. Chief VanBenschoten has told me you have learned well and show promise as future gunners in the Naval Armed Guard. Today, you will be going by train to the Naval Armed Guard Center in Brooklyn, New York. From there, you will be assigned your ships. That is all."

"Attention," called out Silverio. He saluted the commander, who returned the salute, then left in the jeep, again driven by the Chief. The Chief said nothing as they drove away.

"Poor bastards," he thought. "Suicide duty. Most of them probably won't make it past the first ship they're on."

"Okay men," said Silverio, who had been handed the sheaf of papers from the C.O. "Listen up. Here are your orders. I'll call out your names. Take your orders, then go inside and pack your sea bags. A bus will be here in one hour to take you to the train station in Norfolk. Good luck."

With that brief ceremony, and no patriotic speeches, Whitey and his crewmates started their careers in the Naval Armed Guard.

CHAPTER 15

The letter had come from Catskill, been forwarded to Camp Shelton, and finally caught up to Whitey at the Armed Guard Center in Brooklyn. His mother wrote:

Dear Whitey:

Jeff and Alex have enlisted in the Navy. They have been sent to Sampson, which is up in Geneva, N.Y. I thought they would be drafted into the Army, but their draft numbers did not come up.

Will wants to go into the marines, but with your father gone all the time, I need someone around here to take care of things. He keeps pestering me, and your father says we should sign the papers.

We miss you here in Catskill. Will you be able to come home at all?

love,

Your mother

His mother was way behind in the news, thought Whitey. He knew he should write her and tell her of meeting with Jeff and Lex, but he was a terrible correspondent. His musings were interrupted by the sudden blare of the public address system in the cavernous Armed Guard auditorium, where hundreds of men slept, their bunks two high. There was scarcely room to walk between the beds, and sometimes the men had to crawl over other sailor's bunks to reach their own.

"Now hear this! Now hear this! All men listed for the S.S. Fulton Truesdale will report to gate two at 0700."

The Truesdale would be Whitey's first merchant ship and the beginning of his Armed Guard duty.

He would remember the moment the rest of his life, and it was one of his most pleasant memories. He carried his sea bag on his shoulder, and went up the gangway to the ship. To him, the vessel was immense, although it was small in comparison to some of the tankers plying the world's oceans.

At the top of the gangway stood his new commanding officer, Ensign Simpson. Simpson was newly-commissioned, with no sea duty at all. He'd recently completed his officer candidate school at New York University and had finished a short Armed Guard training session in Dam Neck, Virginia, where Whitey had done some of his own training.

Ensign Simpson took his responsibilities seriously. His single gold bar fairly gleamed. His haircut was strictly to Navy regulations, and his tie was knotted properly and set neatly between the points of his crisp starched white shirt. Simpson's blue eyes squinted at the world through gold-rimmed glasses. He drew himself up to his full five foot six and held his hand up as Whitey started past him.

"Sailor -- you don't come aboard my ship unless you do it properly. Is that clear?"

Whitey blinked. Was this little twerp serious? What the hell, this wasn't a Navy ship. It was just a rusty old merchantman. He suppressed a laugh, then went back down the gangway and did as Ensign Simpson had ordered.

"Request permission to come aboard, sir," he said.

"Permission granted," said Ensign Simpson. "Sailor, give your name to Salvucchi here, and then report to gunner's mate first class Kennedy, at the gun mount. It appears to me that your naval etiquette needs some work. Believe me, sailor, by the time I'm through with you, you're going to be sharp, really sharp. I demand proper routine aboard my ship."

Whitey gave his name to the seaman standing with the Ensign, then walked toward the stern gun mount, where he saw a group of men gathered.

Captain Christensen, the grizzled Norwegian master of the Truesdale, had watched from the bridge as Whitey came aboard.

"His ship? Did you hear that, Mr. Walker? That bald-headed young 90-day wonder says it's his ship. I've wrung more sea water out of my skivvies than he's ever sailed on. Damn, I hope I can keep from throwing the little bastard over the side."

Mr. Walker, the ship's first mate, laughed. He looked forward to seeing Captain Christensen put the little shit in his place.

CHAPTER 16

Will Houston was a rugged individualist and marched to his own drummer. Everyone in town expected him to follow his brothers into the Navy, but he had other plans.

Whether it was because his brothers had chosen the Navy or his neighbors expected him to do likewise, no one ever knew, but he told his parents he wanted to be a Marine.

He wanted revenge for what had happened to his brother Jack. He didn't care if the revenge was exacted on the Germans or the Japanese. They were both at war with America. The thought of close combat with the enemy was very satisfying to him, and the Marine Corps would give him that. Their specialty was landing on hostile territory, and had been, since the days of the American Revolution.

Will knew that the Japanese fleet had been virtually destroyed the year before and that the U.S. had begun the "island hopping" strategy that would eventually carry American troops to the very shores of Japan. If he could get into the Marines he'd be a part of that, maybe even send some Japanese to their ancestors.

In early February of 1943, Will Houston got the written permission of his father, since he was still only seventeen, and took a bus to Albany, where he filled out enlistment papers and passed the physical examination for the Marine Corps. Mrs. Houston was in tears when he left. She was against Will's enlistment from the beginning, but Floyd Houston was determined that all of his sons would serve, in one way or another. Floyd had not been able to serve in World War I, due to a heart murmur, and had always felt guilty about this fact. Perhaps his sons' service would make up, in some small way, for what he had not been able to do.

Will got a bus ticket in Albany for New York City. There, he would be joined by other new Marine recruits and sent by train to Charleston, South Carolina, and then by bus to the Marine Corps Recruit Depot at Parris Island.

His training was to be the toughest ordeal he had ever been through, but he would complete it and proudly wear the Marine Corps uniform, twelve weeks later. His brothers would not learn that he was a marine for many months.

CHAPTER 17

Jeff and Lex Houston finished their boot camp in March of 1943, expecting to be assigned to the same duty station or ship, but the loss of the five Sullivan brothers the previous November changed all that.

The Sullivan brothers had enlisted in the Navy in Waterloo, Iowa, and were serving aboard the cruiser U.S.S. Juneau. The bloody battle of Guadalcanal had begun with U.S. Marines launching the first offensive against the Japanese in the Pacific, with landings on Tulagi, Gavitu and Tanambogo, all islands of the Solomon chain. In November of 1942, the Japanese launched a fierce land and sea counterattack, to dislodge the American forces. The U.S. Fleet won a complete victory, but with heavy losses, including the Juneau. Public outcry at the deaths of the five Sullivans resulted in the Navy forbidding brothers to serve on the same ship.

The two Houston brothers were assigned to training for the Armed Guard, their choice, since their brother Whitey had gone that route. When they received their orders, Jeff found that he was going to Camp Shelton, in Virginia, and Lex to San Diego, in California.

Jeff knew that Whitey had just left Shelton a month or so before, according to a letter from his mother, but neither he nor Lex had heard anything about San Diego. Secretly, Jeff envied Lex, because California sounded like good duty, and the weather there was supposed to be pleasant.

Both brothers caught the same train to New York City, where they spent the night in crowded bunks at the Armed Guard Center in Brooklyn. To their amazement, they met Whitey in the chow hall and found that he was awaiting his first ship.

"What's Camp Shelton like, Whitey?" asked Jeff.

"Shelton is a swamp," replied Whitey. "But the weather is getting better now, and it won't be bad. You won't get any liberty, and if Chief Van Benschoten's still there, you'll work your damn butt off -- and you'll learn how to load and shoot. That's what it's all about, Lex. And when the training's all over, you'll soon find yourself on some merchant ship, with fifteen or twenty others, hoping the krauts or Japs don't blow you out of the water. That's what I'll be doing, very shortly. I'm waiting for my first ship. I can hardly believe it."

"Whitey," asked Lex, "have you heard anything about San Diego?"

"Dago -- yeah. They tell me it's A-1 duty. A new station, and warmer than the east coast. They say the chow is great, too. Dammit guys, I'm tickled pink that we got together. A really lucky break!"

The three could not leave the center, but talked late into the night. They did not know it, but this was the last time they would ever be together.

The next morning, after a typical hearty Navy breakfast of coffee, sausages and pancakes at the center's chow hall, Jeff and Lex shook hands with Whitey and then climbed aboard busses for their respective trains.

CHAPTER 18

The weather out on the Atlantic during that week in March of 1943 was horrific. The Fulton Truesdale steamed toward England, carrying a cargo of jeeps and other military hardware. The ship pitched and rolled and all of the Armed Guard crew was seasick, including Ensign Simpson. The convoy had not been troubled by submarines, perhaps because of the fierce seas and poor visibility.

Whitey had never been sicker in his life, not even after a serious drinking spell. Because of the violent rocking and rolling of his ship, no normal meals were served in the galley. The men ate cold cereal and drank coffee, their bodies wedged against bulkheads, to prevent being thrown about the compartments.

"Take my advice," said Whitey's buddy, Tony Salvucchi, "get some bread and smear it with mustard, then gag it down. It will settle your stomach."

Whitey tried it, but ended up being sicker than before. There was no cure for him.

He had been topside and seen the bow half of another merchant vessel, which had broken in half during the storm. The word was that all the survivors of the mishap were on the stern half of the ship, drifting several miles from the bow. He never found out if the men were rescued, but there was nothing anyone could do about it. All hands had all they could do to keep their ships steaming ahead.

On the fourth day the sun miraculously broke through the clouds and the seas calmed, and with the clearing of the stormy skies came the German submarines.

The Truesdale had lost its two port side lifeboats in the storm. They had been smashed by waves and the pieces washed away, but the ship was lucky, compared to the tanker H. H. Rogers. It took a torpedo amidships. The explosion caused water to get into the ship's fuel, and flooded the engine room. The captain ordered "abandon ship," and the vessel started down at the stern. All hands were later rescued.

As quickly as the submarine attack had begun, it ended. No one knew why. Perhaps the subs were short of torpedoes -- this was a common occurrence in the early days of the war -- or Admiral Dönitz had other work for them, more important convoys to attack.

The convoy continued its voyage to England, and the ships passed the debris of many sunken and unknown merchant vessels. Lifeboats, rafts, trunks, clothes, shoes, but no sign of life. The experience did nothing for Whitey's morale and it was a grim notice of what the men of the Armed Guard and their merchant shipmates might expect.

At long last, the convoy arrived in Liverpool. The merchant vessels of the group moored, anchored, docked and unloaded their cargo. Whitey had now become a veteran of the submarine war. Why his ship had been spared when others had been sunk or damaged, he did not know. Altogether, twelve merchant vessels and a hundred merchant seamen and Armed Guard crewmen had been lost on the voyage.

Whitey and Salvucchi took their first shore liberty in a foreign port and drank themselves nearly unconscious. They saw Ensign Simpson, Mr. Walker and Captain Christensen in one of the bars they visited. Simpson seemed to be well on his way to a first-class drunk and the merchant Captain and Mr. Walker seemed amused by the whole thing.

Salvucchi and Whitey met two prostitutes in a bar and spent a few hours with the first ladies of the evening in their young lives. In the following months Whitey would become an old hand at finding and "romancing" women in ports all over the world. Years later he would marvel that he'd never caught a "dose" or any sort of venereal disease. The Lord must watch over young sailors, as well as drunks and mad men, he thought.

CHAPTER 19

HMS Pennywort, a former American four-stacker destroyer, among a host of old ships President Roosevelt had turned over to Great Britain months earlier, steamed around the American convoy that had just been attacked by a German sub. The Submarine had been chased off, but not before it had managed to send a torpedo into the SS Oglethorpe, the first Liberty ship built in Savannah, Georgia. The Oglethorpe had left Savannah weeks before, taking a short detour to New York, where it was loaded with meat, airplanes and trucks, in addition to its original cargo of ammunition. From New York, the ship, with a crew of forty-four merchant seamen and an Armed Guard contingent of thirty men, joined a convoy of other vessels, leaving the first week of May 1943.

The torpedo had penetrated the #1 hold, exploding and then igniting a fire in the cargo. Quickly, the merchant sailors extinguished the blaze. Miraculously, the ship's engines continued to function. The damage had been confined to the ship's forward spaces. The ship's captain took stock of his situation and determined that at least 43 of his crew had abandoned ship sometime during the fire. He set a new course for St. John's, Newfoundland.

Unknown to the captain, eight of his crew had not abandoned ship, but were blown overboard by the force of the explosion. Among these was Jeff Houston.

The Pennywort had thrown a cargo net over the floating men and hauled them aboard. A check of the men's pulses indicated that all were dead, so they were laid at the ship's stern and covered, to be disposed of at the next light.

Early the next morning the British corpsmen pulled the canvas off the eight bodies and began removing their dog tags, wristwatches and billfolds.

"Hey, mate," said one of the corpsmen to his buddy, "this one's moving!"

Of the eight men, two were still alive. These sailors were quickly taken below to the sick bay, and their six shipmates were "consigned to the deep."

"Houston, is it?" asked the British doctor.

"Yes, sir," said Jeff, haltingly. "There was a blast and me and my buddy got blown into the water. Where am I? I was swimming around, swallowing sea water -- there were a bunch of us together, all of us bobbing up and down --"

"Calm down, sailor, said the Doctor. "Two of you made it. The others didn't. Your buddy is still unconscious and he's being looked after. Your ship?"

"The SS Oglethorpe. Was it sunk?"

"Not quite, but it's been badly damaged and it's leaving the convoy, heading for Newfoundland. You're going to be with us for a few days. We're going to Glasgow, Scotland and then on to Liverpool. You're going to be okay, but my guess is that you'll spend some time recovering."

Jeff's recuperation from the sinking was quicker than his Navy doctors expected. The young sailor was tough.

He was checked out of the Navy sickbay in Liverpool in three weeks, and assigned to another ship, the S.S. Whitmore. His buddy had been injured more seriously than he, and was shipped back to the states on HMS Queen Elizabeth.

Although he did not know it, Jeff had been more fortunate than the remaining members of the Oglethorpe's crew. On its way to Newfoundland, the ship was ambushed by another German submarine, which sent her to bottom with two torpedoes. All hands were lost.

Jeff's new commanding officer in the Armed Guard crew of the Whitmore was Lieutenant Allen, an old-time Navy hand and a mustang.

Lieutenant Allen welcomed Jeff aboard his new ship.

"We're glad to have you, Houston. Your record shows you took your training at Camp Shelton -- that's where I took mine, by god. That place must be the asshole of the East Coast -- runs Norfolk a close second. Is Chief VanBenschoten still doing his thing there? He's a tough bastard, but a good man."

"Yes, sir, Chief VanBenschoten is still there, but they told me he's being transferred to Treasure Island soon."

"Okay, Houston. You'll hear this from the rest of the crew, but I'd rather tell you myself. I'm a former gunner's mate -- career man. Got myself a direct commission. I know guns. And I want my men to be the best in the damn Armed Guard. We practice plenty, and god help any krauts who cross our path. I demand your best, and the crew expects it of everyone. We've earned the respect of the merchant crew on the Whitmore and that's not easily come by. If you don't measure up, you'll answer to me. Understood?"

"Yes, sir, understood," said Jeff.

"By the way, Houston, I'm happy to have a veteran with us -- a man who's gone through one sinking. I've been put in the water myself, twice. I look on you as a kind of rabbit's foot for us."

Jeff didn't know what to make of this, but he saluted and returned to his quarters.

CHAPTER 20

Sailors dream of the perfect ship that they will serve in: a modern, large, and magnificent vessel, with comfortable quarters, the latest facilities, and good food.

Lex Houston's first assignment as an Armed Guard gunner was just the opposite, the SS Virginian, an old ship launched in 1904. It was built as a coal-burner, then converted over to diesel power. To Lex, it was a huge disappointment. And so was the cargo it was carrying.

Diego Garcia, a wiry little Puerto Rican steward who had been a merchant mariner for over thirty years, was talking to Lex, who, for some reason, he had befriended.

"We carry horse-food, Houston. Many bushels of oats and straw. I talk to Israel Malenkov -- he is deck hand. He has job of shoveling manure every day. You think he likes this? Never have I sailed on a ship with a cargo like this. Es verdad!"

The ship carried a cargo of six hundred and one mules, loaded onto the vessel in Long Beach and destined for New Guinea, where the mountainous terrain forbid the use of jeeps and armored personnel carriers. The mules were the only way that the Army's field artillery could be moved into position in that area.

The ship was slow and the Navy routed it in what appeared to be a very haphazard way. As a result, the trip took three months, and the normally poor dispositions of the mules got even worse.

The only saving grace of the trip was that the ship had not been attacked by a Japanese submarine or surface vessel. Probably part of the reason for this was that the Virginian had been accompanied on part of its voyage by a Navy destroyer, although for what reason, Lex could only guess.

When the living cargo was off-loaded in Port Moresby, New Guinea, the mules, once their hooves landed on solid ground, panicked and stampeded, dragging their handlers behind them. The scene resembled a riot and the merchant seamen did a poor job of controlling the beasts. After all, they were afraid of the animals.

Lex shook his head, wondering what kind of a Navy he had signed up for. What in hell would he tell his friends back in Catskill about his war experiences, when this was all over? What kind of honor rubs off on a poor sailor when he has the job of protecting a cargo such as this? Lex made up his mind to forget this first assignment.

CHAPTER 21

Jeff Houston's ship, the SS Harvey Whitmore, was at Gibraltar on the fourth of July in 1943. There was no Independence Day celebration there, of course, it being a British-controlled port. The Brits still did not like to talk about that unpleasant period of history.

Jeff was a witness to history this day. Wladyslaw Sikorski, the Premier of the Polish government in exile, died in the fiery crash of his aircraft, less than a mile from where it had taken off. Sikorski had been a thorn in the side of the British, ever since he claimed the Russians had been responsible for the massacre of Polish Army officers in Katyn Forest the previous year. Rumor had it that the British had arranged his death, because he was endangering Russian-American-English "solidarity" in a critical period of the war. Stalin was enraged at Sikorski's allegations, which have since been proven correct.

Did the British have Sikorski killed? No one knows, to this day.

Jeff could not help but see the frantic activity around Gibraltar that day. Planes took off frequently from its airfield and blinker messages constantly winked between the ships in the harbor.

The scuttlebutt aboard the Whitmore was that they were to be sent somewhere in the vicinity of Sicily, to support an invasion.

The scuttlebutt was right. Later that month, the Allied forces invaded what Winston Churchill called "The soft underbelly of Europe," Italy. Landings were made on the island of Sicily by almost 470,000 troops. They were opposed by 60,000 Germans. Jeff's ship took part in the invasion, landing jeeps, ammunition and rations, via LCVP's on the beach.

The Germans, hopelessly outnumbered, began a quick retreat and two -thirds of their force, along with their equipment, were able to escape back to the mainland of Italy. The rest were either killed or captured. The battle took American, Canadian and British forces only thirty-eight days to complete and resulted in the downfall of dictator Benito Mussolini's government. A few weeks later, Italy surrendered to the Allies. The allies had successfully begun the invasion of Europe, but their next landing, at Salerno on the Italian mainland, would not be such a cakewalk.

Jeff felt like a old-hand now. He'd survived one sinking already and he and his shipmates had been initiated into the ranks of the veterans of armed invasion. It looked like nothing could stop Uncle Sam now.

CHAPTER 22

The Armed Guard gun crew were sitting in their gun tub, on the stern of the SS Noordam, swapping sea stories. The Noordam was a massive former ocean passenger liner, and had a big Armed Guard crew, forty-eight men in all. The ship had unusual duties, carrying pilots, Women's Army Corps (WAC) personnel, and nurses, to New Guinea, in the Pacific. The ship was armed heavily, bow and stern. The men considered it good duty and the food and quarters were top notch.

"When I first came aboard," said Carlo Bitonte, a third class gunner's mate from Philadelphia, "I was kind of green. They told me we were going to pass a special "mail buoy", floating somewhere out in the Pacific. They said we could drop off our mail at this buoy, and the next ship heading back stateside would pick it up at the buoy for us. I stayed up all night writing letters home -- to my girl friend, my folks, and my sister back in Philly. The next day they told me I had the watch, to spot that mail buoy. I went on my watch station on the bow, and kept my eyeballs peeled all day. Never did see the damned thing. Everyone had a laugh at my expense."

"Take a gander at this," said Lex Houston, who had come aboard the ship after his first ship, the SS Virginian, returned to the states. He held up a book of matches, imprinted with the letters `ISR.' "I got them from a Filipino merchant sailor back in Long Beach. That friggin' clown MacArthur had these printed up last year when the Japs kicked his ass out of the Philippines. Stands for `I Shall Return.' They say he had cigarette packs and Ronson lighters marked the same way, and gave them out to the Filipinos when he left. What a damn actor -- he should be in the movies."

The others all laughed. MacArthur didn't get much respect from the Navy. Admiral William "Bull" Halsey and Admiral Chester Nimitz were the heroes of the enlisted men, and they'd do anything for these two.

"Hey, have you seen the new JG we just got aboard?" asked Bill Klosterman, a first class gunner. "He's a damned movie actor, name of Henry Fonda. A reserve ninety-day wonder, but not a bad guy, they say, not that I've had any business with him. The old man is busy kissin' his ass. Unusual for him -- he hates us AG people. Thinks we're bad luck for him. But he'd change his tune, believe me, if we came under fire, and had to blast some jap planes out of the sky."

The men all nodded agreement. Every AG aboard had run into at least some hostility from merchant officers, but the merchant crews usually were friendly. They knew that they could count on the Armed Guard people to defend them, when it came to that, and some of the merchant sailors even volunteered to take part in the gunnery practices.

One thing the ship did not have to worry about was submarines, because of its speed. It was capable of better than twenty knots, and the Japanese submarines could not match that when they were submerged. As a result, the ship always sailed alone.

Later in the year, the men would see their ship loaded with casualties to be taken back to the states for treatment, as a result of the island-hopping campaign being waged in the Pacific.

Lex was enjoying his tour of duty on the Noordam.

CHAPTER 23

The Whitmore, with Jeff Houston aboard, was proceeding back to Gibraltar, in August of 1943.

Late in the day on the 13th of that month, a large formation of German bombers approached the convoy that the Whitmore was steaming in. They came in low above the water, with the sun at their backs, to make anti-aircraft defense difficult.

General quarters had already been sounded, and Jeff and the rest of his crew were at their stations. The bombers were met with a deadly hail of fire, causing the attacking planes to alter their plan of assault. Jeff's crew managed to account for one of the planes and two others were blown out of the sky by gunners from other ships. The attack lasted only ten or fifteen minutes, and then the planes were gone.

One of the other ships of the convoy had been struck amidships by a torpedo launched by one of the German planes. A huge hole was blown in the ship, but it did not sink. The hold ruptured by the torpedo contained drums of gasoline, but for some strange reason, they did not explode. A tow line was later rigged and the ship was eventually towed to port by an accompanying destroyer.

Some of the merchant vessels were rigged with torpedo nets. These nets were strung from fore-and-aft booms and were intended to catch incoming torpedoes. The booms were swung outward from both sides of the ship, and the nets were supposed to protect the ship down to the keel. There was never any information as to the effectiveness of these nets, and the merchant captains complained that they slowed the ship, making it difficult to maneuver in convoy.

Few of the other ships of the convoy were damaged, once again proving the effectiveness of the Armed Guard gunners. The death and destruction dealt by their anti-aircraft salvos significantly changed the battle strategy of the German Luftwaffe.

Jeff was beginning to feel like a battle-hardened veteran and he wondered how his two brothers were doing aboard their ships. His only news of them came the long and circuitous route of letters from home, and they contained old news and no detailed information. He did know, though, that his youngest brother Will had joined the marines. This information puzzled him, but then he really did not know what drove Will. He never would.

As the convoy proceeded to Gibraltar, the strains of a newly-popular ballad, *Comin' In On A Wing And A Prayer* drifted out of the ship's radio shack, where the radioman was tuning the bands for news of the war and came across a broadcast by the Armed Forces Radio Network. Jeff liked the tune -- it had a melancholy air to it, and he attempted to hum along. He had long ago learned that you took your pleasure where you could find it these days.

CHAPTER 24

The British Eighth Army, under Montgomery, invaded southern Italy in September of 1943. The Italians had already surrendered and then joined the allies. On the ninth of September, an Allied invasion fleet, the largest assembled up to that point in the war, and covering a thousand square miles of the Tyrrhenian Sea, approached Salerno.

Several powerful German Panzer divisions immediately attacked the landing Allies, but Salerno was taken, and the Allied Air forces pounded the Germans, until they were forced to back off.

Jeff's ship, the Whitmore, took part in this invasion, and carried jeeps and ammunition to the American Fifth Army, commanded by General Mark Clark. The Whitmore's gunners were able to add one more attacking German plane, a dive bomber, to their list of kills.

At this point in the war, duty aboard Armed Guard vessels was highly desired. The merchant ships were new and more comfortable and the armaments carried by them were of the latest design. Sailors were known, in those days, to decline promotions to higher ratings, in order to stay aboard their ships. Anyone making first class petty officer could be expected to be transferred to the Fleet.

Jeff was talking to his buddy, Harvey Kessler, a third class gunner's mate.

"Have you heard the scuttlebutt, Jeff?" asked Kessler.

"I know what you're going to say. They say a Liberty ship, the SS Kimball, sailed from Boston a few weeks ago, and never showed up. It was headed for Liverpool. I knew some guys on that ship. Wonder what happened?"

"The same thing as always happens, Jeff. Some krauts in a sub put a tin fish into her and she's laying on the bottom. Davey Jones' Locker for sure."

"How come we're so lucky, Kessler?"

"Ain't no luck about it, pal. We're mean sons-of-bitches. Any kraut planes or subs come near us, they're gone, believe me."

CHAPTER 25

The SS Noordam was a fast ship, and made many trips among the islands of the Pacific, picking up wounded, dropping off nurses and troops at the far-flung outposts of the U.S. military.

Lex Houston was a little bored. The ship, which could make eighteen to twenty knots, was a difficult target for Japanese submarines, and the Japanese submarine fleet was nowhere as large as Admiral Dönitz's, nor as efficient.

The Noordam usually had recent movies to be shown to the crew. Its "geedunk" always had a good supply of candy and ice cream, and the food aboard was the best anywhere in the Pacific. Yet Lex was becoming unhappy.

One of the reasons he and his brothers had entered the service was to exact some form of revenge on the enemy. Preferably the Germans, who had killed his oldest brother, Jack. Failing this, the next best thing, in Lex's mind, was to take part in some strategically important battle. But his lot seemed to be the mundane job of manning guns aboard a ship that would probably never have to make use of them.

He was out on the ship's huge starboard upper deck one beautiful October night in 1943. The Pacific was calm, the moon was out, and the ship trailed an iridescent wake. The bow of the former luxury liner cut an impressive path through the waves, travelling with "a bone in its teeth" as some of the merchant mariners described it. Bitonte, the gunner's mate, stood alongside Lex. All running lights on the huge vessel were extinguished, but the bright moonlight made it nearly possible to read the print in a newspaper.

"I don't know, Houston, I was scared when they put me into the Armed Guard. We all thought we'd be slugging it out with some submarine or German raider, or maybe fighting off an air attack. But none of that has happened so far. We haven't even seen a Jap submarine. Not that I'm sorry about that -- hell, no! What will I tell my grandchildren about this war? That I spent a good part of it on a blasted luxury liner, ferrying WACs and pilots across the Pacific? This is pretty soft duty. I was thinking the other day that it might not be a bad idea to make a career of the Navy. Back in Philadelphia there weren't too many good jobs when I left. I guess they're building ships at the Navy Yard there, but they tell me that women are doing the riveting, and a lot of the other work. My dad runs a grocery on the south side of town -- and I don't want to go back to that."

"Damn it, Bitonte. I'm a little homesick right now. My girl friend back in Catskill, Fay, hasn't written me -- at least there have been no letters from her. There was a letter from my mother, and that helped. This damn duty is so soft that it gives us all time to think, and that's not a good thing. If we were hell bent on blasting a jap sub out of the water, we wouldn't be in that fix. Dammit, I want some duty where I feel I'm doing something for the war effort -- not like some damn tourist, riding around on a vacation cruise."

"Don't knock it, Houston. One of my buddies, Rudy Gasperian, a guy who went through school at Treasure Island with me, was on the SS Waipo. It was making a run in the northern Pacific -- up near the Aleutians, back in March. He was standing a watch and when his relief came, Rudy was gone. Hell, there was ice on everything, and the sea was high. They figured that he was washed overboard -- and some people said he may have committed suicide. His folks will never know."

Lex nodded, then went below to catch some shuteye.

CHAPTER 26

In November of 1943 Admiral Nimitz, who was in command of the American Central Pacific operations, launched the U.S.'s first offensive in the central Pacific. Marines streamed ashore on the coral atolls of Makin and Tarawa.

Tarawa is actually a coral reef, a string of forty-seven islands, which enclose a lagoon. The atoll is triangular in shape, eighteen miles on its longest side.

The green young marine, frightened at his first amphibious landing, came ashore with his company on an LCVP (Landing Craft, Vehicles & Personnel). The ramp of the craft dropped and the men waded through the surf and quickly took up positions on the coral beach.

At first there was no opposition, and the troops slowly made their way inland, yard by yard. Then the sniper fire began.

Nearly 5000 Japanese were stationed at their garrison on Tarawa and their snipers had been positioned in dense shrubs and shallow trenches not far from where the first marines came ashore.

The young marine dug in and waited. He was more frightened now than when he'd landed, but also curiously excited, now that he had been exposed to enemy fire.

The Japanese sniper, lying hidden in a trench, took a bead on the man, and fired off one round from his rifle. The untested marine was startled when a bullet kicked up sand next to him. He crouched lower in his trench. He neither heard nor felt the second shot, which quickly followed the first.

By this time a marine mortar team had zeroed in on the sniper's position and dropped a round into the trench, blowing the enemy soldier into eternity.

Quickly, the Marine medics crawled to the young marine, but saw that it was too late. The man was dead. One of the corpsmen made a note of the man's dog tag -- W. Houston.

"Christ," said the corpsman, "this kid took a bullet right through his helmet. Damn, he can't be more than seventeen."

Coincidentally, at this same moment back in New York State, Floyd Houston collapsed at the controls of his locomotive, somewhere near Albany, and died of a massive heart attack. The "dead man's control," a safety device on the locomotive's throttle, designed for just such emergencies, slowed and stopped the locomotive.

Back on Tarawa, three days of bloody fighting ensued. The desperate Japanese garrison inflicted heavy casualties on the American forces. So fanatical was the enemy resistance that the Marines wiped out virtually the entire defending force before the islands were secured. Few prisoners were taken.

Admiral Nimitz's forces proceeded northwestward across the central Pacific, invading the Marshall Islands in January of 1944. The fighting to take Kwajalein was as fierce as that which had taken place at Tarawa and Makin, but the military superiority of the American forces prevented supplies and reinforcements from reaching the beleaguered Japanese and the island fell six days after it was invaded.

The American Pacific offensive was underway and the Japanese would not be able to withstand it.

CHAPTER 27

Mrs. Houston's inner strength did not fail her in her double tragedies. She learned of her husband's death from a telephone call and of her son Will's death a week after Floyd's funeral. George Smiley delivered the black-edged telegram from the War Department. The Navy said Will had been buried in a military cemetery on one of the many Pacific islands. His body joined those of thousands of other young marines and sailors who would never see home again.

Mrs. Houston was alone, except for her sister, who lived in Kingston, not many miles away. It was Mrs. Houston who made the funeral arrangements with the minister at the Methodist church in Catskill, and with the Catskill undertaker. Mr. Houston was buried in his family plot, just outside of town. There was a space alongside his grave for Emma, for when that time came. Emma Houston's sister Helen had come to Catskill to stay with her, and to give her sister support, but there was not much that she could do.

Perhaps it was the strain of the loss in quick succession of her oldest son Jack, her youngest, Will, and her husband, but Emma resigned as organist and choir director at the church. The members of the church were very understanding and the minister, Reverend Cudahy, came around to her house after the funeral and talked to her for several hours.

"Mrs. Houston," he said, "death is a part of life, like it or not. But God tells us that the powers of death shall not prevail against his church. And I know that you are a woman of great faith, and that these terrible events in your life will not lessen that faith. God will not ask you to bear more than you are able to, he tells us in the Bible."

Mrs. Houston did not reply to that statement, but sat there quietly, drinking the coffee that she had made for herself and Reverend Cudahy.

But forever after this, she would not be the same woman, and she stopped attending the Sunday services at the Catskill Methodist church.

CHAPTER 28

Bari, Italy is an obscure Italian port on the Adriatic Sea. In December of 1943, Whitey Houston found himself in Bari, on a relatively new Liberty ship, the SS Howard Stone. He had picked up the ship in September, and made a number of uneventful runs to Italian cities, during the early days of the Allies' European invasion of Italy.

The S.S. Howard Stone was built in April of that year, at a brand-new shipyard in Wilmington, North Carolina, Whitey had been told by one of the crew when he first came aboard. They were moored just off Bari's seawall, waiting to offload their cargo of gasoline and explosives.

Bari is located on the east coast of Italy, on the upper heel of the Italian peninsula, almost one hundred miles due east of Naples, across the country. Whitey had been on liberty in Naples while the ship unloaded ammunition and supplies, and a girl in a Neapolitan bar had told him Naples was on the Adriatic sea, but most of the seamen aboard the Stone considered it all part of the Mediterranean.

For once, Whitey found himself in a safe harbor, away from the German submarines and surface raiders, and had been ashore at Bari for a short liberty, immediately after they'd arrived there. The Italians were friendly, the food was good, and the many sailors in Bari were enjoying themselves. The Armed Guard gun crew thought they could relax, but their officer, a young Ensign from Milwaukee, was gung ho, insisting on constant training and the men had begun to feel a bit cranky at what they considered too much spit and polish.

The British Eighth Army was driving north in Italy, against heavy German opposition, and there were nearly thirty freighters and tankers here in Bari's harbor, waiting to unload their much-needed cargoes. All incoming supplies were immediately loaded onto trucks and then driven north, to be used by General Montgomery's advancing forces.

Whitey and his buddy from New Orleans, the huge and hulking cajun Charlie Chanson, who everyone called Charlie Chan, were playing cards and sitting on their bunks.

"Ensign Hardaway is doing it the hard way, as usual," said Charlie. "Lordy, Whitey, these 90-day wonders sometimes get to me. I think we could teach that fuzzy-cheek a few things about gunnery."

"I don't know, Charlie. Ensign Hardass isn't really such a bad guy. He just wants to do things right, and the old man and the first mate are giving him a tough time, young as he is. You know how these merchant guys are with every new officer we get, until they get to know him."

"Shit fire," said Charlie, "I'm getting a headache, cooped up down here. Let's go topside and take the air."

The two men tossed their playing cards on Whitey's bunk and pulled on their peacoats. It was cold outside and the damp air would go through to a man's bones, chilling him thoroughly.

The sailors had just emerged from a hatch on the starboard side of the ship when bright flares, suspended beneath parachutes, began floating down from the sky. At first, they were beautiful, like fireworks in a fourth of July celebration. The sound of planes could be heard, although none could be seen. The General Quarters alarms broke the calm of the winter night, and Whitey and Charlie shed their peacoats, pulling on lifejackets as they did so. Quickly, the rest of the gun crews manned their positions and waited for orders from Ensign Hardaway.

GQ could be heard from the other ships moored by the seawall and men scurried to their anti-aircraft guns on the other ships, but no firing had yet started.

"Captain Fitchner, I know we're supposed to wait for the signal from the shore batteries to commence firing, but I think we should begin now," said Ensign Hardaway, who was on the bridge with the Captain.

"I agree," said Fitchner, the grizzled old master of the Stone. "Go to it."

Ensign Hardaway passed the word via the ship's speakers, and the gun crews on the Stone were the first of the ships to send their curtain of death skyward. Every sixth shell fired from the 20 millimeter Oerlikons was a tracer, drawing bright lines across the sky. Almost at once, twenty merchant vessels' Armed Guard gun crews began firing.

With startling suddenness, an explosion rocked the ship, then a second and a third. Bombs had hit holds one, three and five, and fires broke out. An object flew through the air from one of the explosions and struck Whitey in the left arm and he lost the feeling there. Blood flowed down his shirt sleeve, and he was confused and frightened. Someone had fallen across his legs, knocking him to the deck, and he saw that it was Charlie, but Whitey's battery continued firing.

The ship was on fire from stem to stern and Captain Fitchner, an experienced mariner with the full knowledge that his ship contained high explosives and gasoline, gave the order to abandon ship. The Stone began to list heavily to port, an indication that she was quickly taking on water. Ensign Hardaway hastily mustered six men from his AG crew and rushed belowdecks to find injured crewmen. The men returned, dragging and carrying a half dozen others. Lifeboats were launched from the Stone and the men rowed to the nearby seawall. The young ensign and the merchant seamen assisted their injured shipmates out of the boats and Captain Fitchner and Ensign Hardaway began a muster.

In the distance, the SS Howard Stone sank slowly beneath the surface of the harbor. Flaming oil and gasoline covered the area where it had been.

"Dammit, Dammit," said the Captain, "There goes my ship. I'm missing four men, and we've got a couple of dozen badly wounded."

"Four of my people didn't make it to the boats," replied Hardaway. He seemed on the verge of tears and the Captain felt deep pity for the young man.

With a tremendous roar, an explosion ripped through one of the ships still at anchor, obviously one that had been loaded with a cargo of ammunition. The concussion knocked those on the seawall off their feet and the air was filled with flying steel and wood. Ensign Hardaway, alive just moments before, lay dead across the concrete blocks of the bulkhead, his skull pierced by a jagged piece of steel plate which had been hurled into the sea wall by the force of the blast.

The other ships in the harbor were sitting ducks. One by one they were hit by bombs, dropped by the low-flying Focke-Wulf 200's and the higher-flying Dorniers. Occasionally a Heinkel would come roaring in, releasing a torpedo at wave-top level.

By some unexplained quirk of fate, the entire harbor was illuminated by a searchlight from ashore, and an allied anti-aircraft battery began firing at one of the merchant vessels, the SS Samuel J.Tilden, killing and injuring some of the crew. The German aircraft finished off the job and sent the ship to the bottom of the harbor, in an explosive burst of burning ammunition and gasoline.

One of the Liberty ships, the S.S. John Harvey, unknown to most of its crew and their Captain, carried 100 tons of World War I type mustard gas. Only the Army chemical-warfare personnel aboard knew of the cargo. Several bombs from the German attackers struck the ship, causing the vessel to explode, and all aboard were killed, either by the explosion or the release of the deadly yellow cloud of poison gas. No one with knowledge of the ship's fatal cargo was left alive to warn others. The air that night was calm, so the cloud was slow to spread.

Ambulances and any other vehicles that could be commandeered, were used to carry the dead and wounded to a field hospital which had been set up just outside Bari. Whitey was in this group, and the action surely saved his life.

Slowly, the deadly cloud spread over the city. Before the week was over, 600 Allied soldiers, sailors and merchant seamen, and hundreds of Italian civilians would be dying as a result of exposure to the lethal fumes. The convoy had been poorly prepared for the attack. The allied officers in charge of the port of Bari were unaware that Major General Peltz, the German air commander in the Balkans, had learned of the convoy's arrival, hours earlier, and planned a surprise attack on the port. German reconnaissance planes had made a circuit of the area a few hours before, but, unbelievably, few in command attached much importance to this fact.

Back in the United States, the War Department immediately issued orders for the incident to be covered up. A few months before, President Roosevelt had authorized the stockpiling of the gas, to be used if the Germans resorted to the use of chemical warfare. These facts would not become public knowledge until more than thirty years later.

The Bari raid lasted twenty minutes and cost the allies seventeen ships. The British 8th Army's campaign on the Italian peninsula was seriously stalled as a result of the terrible loss of men and materiel. This disaster was the most costly battle of the war for the Naval Armed Guard.

And Whitey Houston lay recuperating in a field hospital outside Bari, with a wound from a one-inch piece of shrapnel in his left elbow. It would pain him for the rest of his life.

CHAPTER 29

-1944-

Whitey, slowly recovering from his wounded elbow, had been put on a destroyer and sent to Loch Ewe, in Scotland. Loch Ewe was one of two hopping-off points for the merchant ships making the dreaded Murmansk run to Russia, a 1500-mile voyage. On his arrival in Scotland, he received a surprising set or orders.

A gunner's mate on the S.S. Wooldridge N. Ferris had suffered a burst appendix and was in sick bay. The gun crew was already short-handed and Whitey, though not completely recovered from his wound, was the replacement. He was quickly transferred to the Ferris. One of the Armed Guard crew members told him the scuttlebutt had them scheduled to leave around the 12th of January, although this kind of information was always highly confidential, and closely guarded.

"They say we'll have only about four hours of daylight this trip," said Forstheimer, an older third class gunner's mate. "There's gonna be plenty of snow and ice, and we'll freeze our asses off. They tell me there's pack ice too, and it can punch a hole through your hull. Worse than those damn German U-boats. And the kraut bombers -- they come from airfields in Norway -- if they can't drop a passel of bombs on you, they'll radio your position to some wolf pack nearby. And god help you if you have to take to a life raft -- you're a dead man in those cold waters, in short order."

"Forstheimer, why don't you blow that shit out your ass?" asked Whitey. "You've never made the trip, from what I hear. Neither have I. Everyone always exaggerates that stuff. It can't be that bad."

Forstheimer only shook his head and walked away.

On a foggy January morning the big convoy steamed out of Scotland and immediately came under attack. One of the trailing merchant vessels was torpedoed. The ship listed to starboard and was giving off steam as she was abandoned. One hundred depth charges were thrown into the sea, but the submarines, and they were definitely one of Admiral Dönitz' "wolfpacks," continued to attack. Two more ships were torpedoed, these sinking very quickly, and their crews took to the lifeboats. Not one ship stopped to pick up survivors - to have done so would have made them choice targets. Likewise, any ship experiencing mechanical problems would become a straggler, and a certain candidate for destruction.

The attack ceased às suddenly as it began, and the convoy continued toward Molotovsk, their Russian destination.

German planes flew over daily, some dropping bombs, others probably reporting the convoy's position. The AG gunners poured a rain of steel into the sky when the bombers appeared, and the planes were forced to do their bombing from high altitudes, which proved to be a very unreliable tactic. Once again, the Armed Guard gunners demonstrated their ability to effectively defend their ships against attacks from the sky.

The weather turned ugly, a curse and a blessing at the same time, since the German subs had to contend with it as well. Rain pelted down, sometimes horizontally, driven by a bone-chilling wind off the sea, then followed by sleet and snow. The wind never let up, swinging around from northeast to northwest, and causing the ship's superstructure to sing and vibrate. The waves crashed against the vessel's bow, and the Ferris plunged into the valleys between them, then tried to ride their crests. The vessel's plates creaked and groaned and all hands thanked their lucky stars that the Ferris was riveted, rather than welded. Some of the earlier mass-produced Liberty ships were welded, and had broken in two on this very run.

It was impossible for the men to sit in the galley area and eat. Huge coffee pots were hung from the overhead and the crew braced themselves against any handy vertical support and cradled their bowls, cups and plates in their laps, while they attempted to finish their meals. Food slopped all over the mess decks, and a number of the newer men vomited while trying to eat, which did not help the situation.

Visibility from the Ferris' bridge was unbelievably poor, and the captain and crew were in constant fear of collision with the rest of the convoy. The gun mounts froze, and had to be thawed with acetylene torches. Snow filled the gun tubs, and the ship's rigging was covered with ice. The Armed Guardsmen shoveled out their guns, and the merchant sailors, bundled in heavy clothes and with their faces swathed in mufflers and scarves, climbed the rigging with chipping hammers and worked feverishly at removing the slick ice. If they had not done so, the freighter would have become dangerously top-heavy and prone to threateningly severe rolls. Ships had been known to capsize in such conditions and the more experienced hands knew it, although they chose to remain silent on this fact. Sometimes what you don't know won't hurt you.

Occasionally a ship would strike a floating mine. The explosion would light up the 20-hour-long night, but no one on Whitey's ship knew the fate of the unlucky vessel or its crew. They could only hope the damage was not severe, and a few of the more religious crewmen offered silent prayers for their shipmates and themselves.

On the last day of January, the Ferris arrived alongside the pier at Molotovsk.

CHAPTER 30

The convoy was being unloaded and the men were truly disappointed. Russian sentries were posted at all the gangways and all hands were forbidden from leaving the ship. A sprawling area alongside the piers was being used as a temporary storage depot. Piles of food, clothing, jeeps and ammunition quickly filled the space. Russian women acted as guards at the depot, and from time to time the women loaded a small-gauge railway train with the cargo and the train chugged off, toward the war front.

Whitey occasionally went out on deck. The air was bitter cold and snow seemed to be falling constantly. He noticed that the Russian women in the storage lots had their feet wrapped in brown paper, tied with white cord, to protect them from the snow and cold.

Where the hell were their boots? His imagination always had pictured Russians, men and women both, in boots, with fur hats and ear flaps. These people looked like the vagrants he'd seen in New York City. He felt sorry for them, and wondered why he and the rest of the crew were forbidden to go ashore.

Whitey pulled an unopened pack of cigarettes from his pea coat and flipped it to the base of the gangway, where an old Russian soldier stood. The cigarettes landed at his feet. The soldier glanced up at Whitey, then at the cigarettes, but did not pick them up. He seemed afraid, and looked quickly around. In the rest of the time that Whitey watched, the Russian made no effort to retrieve the pack, and Whitey went back below to get warm.

Down in the crew's quarters, Whitey stopped to talk to one of the merchant crew. The man was a hard-bitten case, and had been in the merchant marine nearly a year. Whitey had seen men like him, wandering the roads and highways, back in New York State. Those men claimed to be hoboes, not tramps or bums. A hobo, they said, would accept work, in return for lodging and food. They objected to being called tramps or bums, who only wanted handouts, without the work.

"How the hell're you making out, kid?" asked the man.

"Not bad, Woody, but it would be great to get ashore and try some of that Russian vodka."

"Fat chance," said Woody Guthrie. "But you don't need to get ashore for vodka. Try this." And he produced a bottle of "Boris' Vodka" and a can of orange juice.

"Where'd you get that?" asked Whitey.

"The Russkis came aboard when we docked. A bunch of them walked through the spaces, inspecting, and I was pickin' out a few tunes on my guitar. They stopped and listened, and one of them gave me this vodka. I gave the guy a carton of Old Golds. He was so pleased he almost hugged me to death. But he was a big-shot. If they catch any of the peasants taking anything from us, their asses would be in a sling."

The two men sat and drank vodka and OJ for an hour and Guthrie told Whitey stories of his experiences, "bummin" around' the U.S. and then joining the Merchant Marine in 1943. He'd been torpedoed twice, and had taken part in three invasions. Whitey was impressed that a civilian like Guthrie could have had so much war experience, in such a short time - but he knew that this man was not your run-of-the-mill deck hand.

Three boring weeks later, most of the convoy was making their way back to Scotland. Although the men didn't look forward to the bad weather and submarine and air attacks, they had their fill of the boredom of sitting alongside a dock in Molotovsk.

Unbelievably, the weather was worse than on the trip to Russia, but because of that, there were no attacks at all. The convoy scattered, unable to maintain signal flag communications, forbidden to use their radios, and the ships were unable to stay together.

In the normal convoy, speed is dictated by the speed of the slowest ship in the group, so the dispersement of the merchant vessels was another blessing in disguise. Whitey's ship was capable of fifteen knots and the return voyage to Scotland passed quickly and without event.

Whitey Houston's Armed Guard career had consisted of a number of lucky breaks. Someone must have been praying for him back home, he often thought.

CHAPTER 31

One of the ports from which merchant vessels formed up for convoys to Russia was Reykjavik, Iceland, and this is where Whitey found himself in late April of 1944.

Reykjavik is on the southwest coast of Iceland, and it was the starting point for a convoy of more than thirty ships, which were to sail for the Russian port of Murmansk. The voyage would take the ships around the southern coast of Iceland, then through the Norwegian sea and north, past the Arctic Circle. They would pass through the Barents Sea, and stop at Murmansk and later, Archangel.

Most of the ships were loaded with strategic and mainly explosive cargo -- high-octane gasoline and high explosives. The convoy was under the command of a Royal Navy Commodore. All convoys going to North Russia were always under the command of a Royal Navy officer, but sometimes included U.S. Naval warships for protection, as was the case this trip. Two U.S. cruisers and two destroyers accompanied the convoy, along with two Royal Navy corvettes, a smaller version of the U.S. "tin cans," but fast and maneuverable.

Whitey was aboard another Liberty ship, the SS Granville Wheeler, recently off the launching ways of Wilmington, North Carolina. He felt comfortable on this vessel. Although of welded construction, the manufacturing kinks which had previously caused Liberty ships to break in two in violent storms, had been ironed out. Another advantage was that Whitey's ship was loaded with jeeps, small arms ammunition, and food stuffs. He'd never felt right aboard a ship carrying high explosives. Those things would go up like a rocket, if hit by a bomb or a torpedo in the right place. In many of these cases, everyone and everything were virtually vaporized by the explosion, and little, if anything, would remain as a clue to the event. Years later, the post-war sea logs of the German U-Boats would provide eloquent testimony as to the fates of many merchant ships which had disappeared without a trace during the war.

The crew knew they could expect more hours of daylight during this trip, and that entailed more danger from German air and sea attacks. The weather was not bad for April, and the Granville's radio man had told the crew that no big storms were expected in the near future.

The Armed Guard gunnery crew was experienced and confident. Their commanding officer was Lieutenant Harry DeMars, a gunnery officer with several years of sea combat behind him.

The convoy had left on a Thursday morning, weather beautiful, seas calm, good visibility. By the second day out, the convoy ran into heavy fog and it stayed with them for nearly fourteen days. The danger of collision was something each ship's master had to keep uppermost in his mind, and the ships of the convoy blew their call letters on their horns, using morse code, to keep track of each other. Watches were doubled out on deck as an extra precaution.

The Armed Guard gun crews aboard the Wheeler made good use of their time, keeping their guns cleaned, holding frequent gun drills and checking their response to General Alarms. Lieutenant DeMars was satisfied that his crew could handle anything that would come their way.

The convoy was seeing fifteen hours of daylight each day. In May this would increase to twenty hours, and they would be much more vulnerable to air attacks.

The fog cleared and the sun shone brightly on the fifteenth day of their voyage. Beautiful white clouds scooted overhead. Whitey and several other members of his gun crew were playing cards in their quarters when their ship was rocked by an enormous explosion. General Quarters was sounded and the men were at their stations in seconds. Flames were shooting from a hold amidships, when a second explosion, much worse than the first, came from the bow.

The men knew that they'd been the victims of at least two torpedoes. The merchant crew was fighting the fires in the amidships hold. Whitey looked up from his gun tub and watched as the bow of his ship slowly turned and went its own independent way. The ship's bow had broken off, leaving the rest of the ship floating free.

The ship's master, Captain Alvarez, checked his situation and saw that the Granville could not remain afloat much longer. Water was streaming into some of the holds and the bilge pumps could not keep up. One of the Navy destroyers made high-speed runs around the convoy, dropping depth charges. None of the other ships of the convoy appeared to have been hit. Perhaps the attack was initiated by a solitary sub, and not the dreaded Wolf Pack. The men hoped that the quick counterattack with depth charges had either scared the boat off, or damaged it.

Meanwhile, Captain Alvarez, fearful of the ship sinking and taking his crew with it, ordered a search below decks for any wounded or unconscious crewmen, then sounded "ABANDON SHIP" over the ship's PA system. It was an orderly function. Lifeboats and life rafts were lowered, and loaded with men. The life rafts were secured to the lifeboats and rowed away from the ship, to avoid the suction as it went down. But the ship remained afloat, although listing heavily to one side.

One of the British corvettes maneuvered carefully alongside the floating caravan of survivors and lowered a cargo net over its side. The able-bodied men clambered up the net, assisting those who were wounded. It was necessary to hoist some of the wounded aboard the British warship via lines secured to their life jackets.

A muster of the crew, once aboard the corvette, revealed that only two men were missing, and these had been amidships at the time of the explosion. They had probably been pulled out of the huge hole in the side of the Granville, following the explosion of the first torpedo.

The corvette made several circuits of the abandoned freighter, looking for floating bodies, or other survivors, but found none. Finally, the corvette shelled the hulk until it sank. The remaining portion of the ship would have been a hazard to navigation and needed to be eliminated.

The corvette returned the men to Loch Ewe, Scotland.

In wartime, trained and experienced sailors are at a premium, so there was to be no rest or recreation for Whitey. He was immediately reassigned to the SS Jean Nicolet, scheduled to make calls along the west coast of Africa, and then to proceed later to the Indian Ocean. Some of the other men were returned to the states on a fast Destroyer Escort, and would then be reassigned.

All of the AG gun crew had survived the sinking of the Granville, and would live to fight again.

As the Nicolet put out from Loch Ewe, the radioman received word of a series of gigantic explosions in the harbor of Bombay, India. A fire had broken out on a ship in the docks, and before it could be brought under control spread to some ammunition, causing a series of fires, explosions and tidal waves. The fires then leap-frogged to adjacent warehouses. The scene had been a nightmare and military authorities were trying to play it down, but bad news travels fast.

More than fifteen hundred people had been killed and better than four thousand injured. Twenty merchant vessels were destroyed and nearly 600 storage buildings were consumed by the holocaust.

Many years later it was revealed that the British merchant vessel which caught fire and triggered the series of horrible events was carrying 1400 tons of ammunition, bales of cotton, thousands of cubic feet of lumber, kerosene, oil, fertilizer, and scrap iron. Secretly hidden in with this cargo were 124 solid gold ingots which had been sent by the Bank of

England to the Reserve Bank of India, to help stabilize the rupee, India's basic currency. Only one of the gold bars was ever recovered. It was found one thousand miles away from the port -- probably picked up by someone who gave up trying to sell it, and abandoned it. The remaining gold bars still rest at the bottom of the murky Bombay harbor, should any would-be treasure hunter wish to attempt a recovery.

The blow to the war effort was staggering. More than 100,000 tons of vitally needed cargo ships were lost, along with millions in war materials. The total loss was later estimated at over one billion dollars.

It was in 1980 that Whitey learned his old boot-camp buddy, Marq LeVesque, from Maine, had been aboard one of those cargo ships in Bombay. Nothing of LeVesque was ever found.

CHAPTER 32

The weather had improved on June 5, 1944 and General Eisenhower made the decision to launch the invasion of Europe the next day. Millions of American, British, Canadian, Free French and other allied troops had been training intensively for this day.

A strip of coastline in Normandy had been chosen for the landings, between Cherbourg and Le Havre. For two days prior to the invasion, the most intense aerial and naval bombardment of World War II had been taking place, in an attempt to soften up the German coastal defenses.

The Allied attack, when it came, involved more than four thousand ships and eleven thousand aircraft. The Germans were unable to put up any kind of significant air defense. The skies belonged to the Allies.

By the second of July, the strategic port of Cherbourg had been captured and a flood of war materiel poured into the European theater. The blueprint for the defeat of the Nazi forces had been set in motion, and the need for ammunition and war materiel would put demands on America's war production and set records for an incredible output of planes, ships, guns, and tanks. Along with this production there would be a need for delivery, which could only be met by the Merchant Fleet, and this need would result in the manning of over six thousand merchant vessels, each with its own crew of Armed Guard gunners, ready to defend against air or surface attack. The merchant ships had become, in reality, warships.

CHAPTER 33

- June 1944 -

It was the damndest sight Lex had ever seen -- five hairy monkeys madly scampering along, aft the starboard deck of the S.S. George Taylor, chasing a sixth, which carried a stalk of bananas. Lex leaped up onto the gun mount, as the five animals reached the ship's stern and stopped short of him.

He'd heard rumors of these creatures being aboard, but no one had actually seen one of them. The ship's radioman, Felix Graham, had told Lieutenant Holmes, the gun crew's commanding officer, that he was convinced there was a monkey hiding somewhere in his compartment. He swore he could sometimes smell it. Small items would disappear forever, and many times packages of cookies, candy and crackers would be torn open and eaten, the empty wrappers tossed on the deck.

Graham said that one night he'd heard stealthy movement in his room. Quickly he flicked on the overhead light, but saw nothing. The next morning there was a depressed spot at the foot of his bunk -- still warm. He'd searched the small area but came up empty-handed. Graham said he was just as happy to find no sign of a monkey because he'd heard the little bastards had a nasty bite.

Lex had thought Graham was full of shit and that the whole thing was his imagination. At the time, Lex had been on the ship only three months and had seen no sign of anything unusual. Perhaps the idea was fueled by information offered by Captain French, who said they'd carried a shipment of 300 Rhesus monkeys through the Panama Canal and up the east coast of the U.S., bound for the polio research labs at Johns Hopkins in Baltimore. Captain French wondered if some of the chimps had gotten loose, but didn't seem to be concerned about it, as long as the ship's work was not hindered.

Lex had come aboard the ship in San Francisco, one beautiful day in May of 1944. The city was number one on his list of favorite ports. Great weather, outstanding liberty and beautiful women. What more could a young sailor ask for?

The Taylor was headed for Pearl Harbor, carrying jeeps and ammunition in its five holds, and was two days out of San Francisco.

"Holy shit, Lex," said Phil Stravinski, the fat young gunner's mate from Chicago, "friggin' monkeys." The blonde sailor could move, in spite of his bulk, and joined Lex on top of the 3-inch 50 caliber cannon.

The two sailors watched with amazed fascination as the six monkeys ran, climbed, leaped and swung their way toward them. The five animals pressing the sixth were after the bananas -- it didn't take a genius to see that, but the sixth monkey was clever and fast and managed to stay just ahead of the others, clutching his prize all the while.

A Liberty ship is over 441 feet long, and this may seem like a great distance, but the six monkeys, which had burst out of a hatch amidships, made it quickly to the gun mount, where Lex and Stravinski clung to the cannon.

The lead monkey, bananas clutched in his right paw, climbed a lifeboat davit, with the others following on his heels. He hesitated when he reached the highest point, then with an impressive leap, cleared the side of the ship, landing with a great splash in the Pacific Ocean. The remaining five monkeys hesitated not one instant, jumping one by one after the lead animal, who by this time was swimming away.

At a speed of eleven knots, the ship soon left the six chimpanzees in its wake.

CHAPTER 34

It was a tremendous change -- duty in the warm Indian Ocean, after the chilling Murmansk runs earlier in the year, and then Mediterranean voyages to and from Italy. After his unexpected assignment to the American Liberty ship SS Jean Nicolet in July off 1944, Whitey found himself making port calls along the west coast of Africa, then trips to Ceylon and India.

The Nicolet had a crew of forty-one, thirty passengers, an Armed Guard contingent of twenty-eight men, and a lone Army medic. It carried general cargo and was sailing from Colombo, in Ceylon, on its way to Calcutta. The ship was not in convoy.

Unknown to the ship's captain, David Nillson, they were being tracked by a Japanese submarine.

Commanding the Japanese submarine I-8, was Commander Tatsunosuke Ariizumi, one of the most sadistic of the World War II Japanese submarine captains.

Ariizumi ordered two torpedoes fired at the Nicolet, both of which struck her on the starboard side. The ship immediately started to take on water and began to list severely. Captain Nillson, realizing that his ship was finished, ordered all hands to abandon ship.

The Japanese submarine surfaced amongst the lifeboats and rafts that had been launched, and rammed one of the lifeboats. Some of the Japanese submarine's crew members then began firing rifles and machine guns at the boats. Finally, the firing stopped.

"Come alongside and come aboard, or you will all be shot," barked an English-speaking Japanese officer, from the submarine's conning tower.

Ninety-six men boarded the sub, and stood on its huge deck. A very few lucky men were on a small raft and managed to paddle away from the submarine, under cover of darkness.

Whitey was among those who were herded onto the deck of the sub.

One of the merchant crew, a young boy of seventeen, began screaming in terror. As a warning, Commander Ariizumi had him shot, and the body was thrown over the side.

For the next four hours, the remaining men were made to run a gauntlet of Japanese sailors. They were pummeled with pipes, rifle butts, pistols and knives, punched, and beaten. Those who fell and did not get up were either left where they lay or shoved into the water.

Finally, the men who appeared to be still alive, were bound together, in groups of four. Their possessions, watches, rings, shoes, belts and dog tags, were taken. They were made to sit forward of the submarine's conning tower, and the men knew they were going to die. Abruptly, the submarine's alarm sounded. Commander Ariizumi's radar had picked up an approaching vessel, and he ordered the boat to crash dive. The Japanese crew scampered back down the conning tower, closed and "dogged" the main hatch, and the submarine disappeared under the waves.

When the submarine had surfaced, hours before, Whitey had instinctively hidden his knife in his sock. It was missed when the Japanese sailors searched him and his shipmates. As he sank, he was able to pull one of his hands free from his bonds. He recovered the knife, then began cutting some of his shipmates free. He did not know how many he had freed, but the water was filled with thrashing bodies.

Fortunately for those who were still alive, the area was littered with pieces of rafts, floating debris from the Nicolet, and even a lifeboat, though it was riddled with machine-gun bullets. Those who were able, pulled themselves aboard anything that would float, then collected as many others as they were able to, fastening them to their floating sanctuaries.

The approaching vessel was a Ceylonese patrol boat, and twenty-four bloody, beaten, and nearly dead survivors of the SS Jean Nicolet were crammed onto the decks of the boat, then taken back to Batticaloa, a small town on the east coast of Ceylon.

It was many days before the men would be back in Colombo, where they were picked up by an American destroyer and eventually returned to England.

The words of Silverio, the gunner's mate back at Camp Shelton, rang in Whitey's ears: "Houston, get yourself a good sharp knife and carry it aboard those merchant ships."

A year later, in August of 1945, Ariizumi, who had been praised by the Japanese military for his "gallantry" in action, committed hari-kari, and was buried at sea. Had he returned to Japan, he would have been tried as a war criminal, and very likely hung or shot.

CHAPTER 35

In July of 1944 the Atlantic Ocean was serene. It was ideal weather for Admiral Dönitz's hunter-killer packs, looking for ships which were not in convoy.

The SS Charles J. Journigan, a brand-new Liberty ship on her maiden voyage, was steaming about 250 miles southwest of the Canary Islands, carrying a cargo of war supplies, including twelve P-38 fighters. Suddenly she was hit by two torpedoes. The damage was great and instantaneous, and her master ordered her abandoned.

Jeff Houston and the rest of his Armed Guard gun crew, along with most of the merchant crew, had plenty of time to make it into lifeboats, as the ship slowly sank beneath the calm waters. Unfortunately, no one in the lifeboats was knowledgeable about small-boat seamanship, and they drifted aimlessly for two days.

The second night they were adrift, a German submarine came up under the group of lifeboats, causing one of the boats to be lifted and stranded high and dry on the stern of the sub.

The German Captain came out on the conning tower and asked in broken English what ship they were from. It would have done no good to decline -- the name of the Journigan was painted on each lifeboat. The men responded.

"So," said the Captain, "you are one of the new Liberty ships. So. That is good."

The Captain spoke in German to one of his crew, and the man disappeared, reappearing moments later with a carton of German cigarettes, which he gave to the men on the boat hung up on the sub's stern.

The men wondered if they would be shot, or taken prisoner, but such was not to happen. The Captain shouted a course for them to steer, disappeared into his conning tower, and the sub submerged.

The lifeboat on the sub's stern floated free.

One week later, the men, in relatively good shape because of their supplies of water and dry crackers, were all picked up by a Portuguese fishing boat some miles off the West African coast. Jeff and his crew mates were eventually returned to the neutral city of Lisbon, Portugal, and flown back to New York City.

Jeff had heard the stories of German and Japanese cruelty, and the experience left him with a sense of bewilderment. These Germans were the same people who had sent his older brother's ship to the bottom, the same people who intended to conquer the world, and establish the Third Reich as the New World Order.

The navy was granting leaves of up to ten days and Jeff boarded a train out of New York, heading for Catskill, where he would visit his mother.

Mrs. Houston and her son sat in the kitchen of her house, drinking coffee.

"Mom," he said, "I don't know what to make of these Nazis. The sailors on that submarine could have killed us all. The Captain of the submarine seemed to be concerned about our safety. I guess his only concern in the war was to sink merchant ships, and killing us wasn't something he wanted on his conscience."

"They're all animals, as far as I'm concerned," his mother said. "They and the Japanese started this thing. Look how many people their bombers have killed in England -- civilians mostly. Hitler certainly doesn't have any compunctions about butchering civilians, if they get in his way."

Jeff was a local hero for that short period in Catskill. After all, he'd been involved in action, his ship had been sunk, and he survived. He'd even come face-to-face with the Germans, and lived to tell about it.

The ten days passed quickly and Jeff Houston returned to the Brooklyn Armed Guard center, to await assignment to his next merchant vessel.

He talked with some other AG's who had heard stories similar to his. A merchant vessel had been torpedoed off Trinidad and sank in six minutes. Seven AG's survived. The submarine which had fired the torpedoes surfaced and picked up several survivors who were filthy and covered with oil. They were taken aboard, cleaned up, given hot tea, rum, cheese and bread. The Captain issued the men a dinghy and a supply of water, and one day's ration of hardtack.

"I wish you well," he said, in heavily accented English. "Your comrades are a few miles south. In any case, continue to head south and you will reach land."

Two days later, the men were picked up by a Brazilian tanker and taken to Brazil.

Jeff was puzzled even more with this new information. He thought that he would never understand human nature, not even if he lived to be a hundred.

Back in Berlin, the stories of the kindness of some of Admiral Dönitz' submarine commanders reached Adolph Hitler and the Fuëhrer flew into one of his famous rages. He ordered Dönitz to call a halt to this, but the Admiral ignored the order. So successful was the Admiral's submarine force, and so respected was he as a naval officer, that he was able to get away with this insubordination, but Hitler continued to fume. In spite of this fact, after the war the Admiral would be tried and convicted of war crimes and sent to Spandau prison for a term of ten years. Probably a point against Dönitz was the fact that Hitler had chosen him to be the Fuëhrer after his suicide.

In 1976 a panel of 400 American and foreign military leaders stated that Dönitz' conviction had been unfair and set a dangerous precedent for war at sea. Rear Admiral Samuel Morrison, the well-known Naval historian, regarded Dönitz as "a capable tactician, who fought fair."

But, "To the victors belong the spoils," as Andrew Jackson once said, and the vanquished of World War II would be severely punished. Had the U.S. lost the war, would Germany and Japan have exacted a much more costly revenge? It is very likely.

CHAPTER 36

In August of 1944 Whitey Houston was in London, waiting to be assigned to another merchant vessel. He was quartered near the West India Dock area, with a dozen other Armed Guard sailors.

One warm and humid evening, quite unusual for London, he and three other AGs were playing poker in their small barracks area, when the air-raid warning sirens sounded.

The air-raid shelter was a cellar directly under the barracks, and the men wasted no time getting there and securing the doors against explosions.

Although the sailors didn't know this, the air-raid was not a conventional one. The Germans had launched what at the time was called "buzz bombs." These devices were crude, slow-travelling rockets, fired from special launching pads in Calais, and other coastal locations in France. Hitler called them V-1's, or "Vengeance Weapons." The rockets emitted a raucous humming note as they flew on their deadly and arbitrary paths.

The force of the explosion from these one-ton rockets was directed horizontally, levelling everything in and around its impact area. The blast never penetrated to any appreciable depth, but the concussion in the horizontal plane was unbelievable.

As the missiles flew into the dock area, they were tracked by British high-powered searchlights and a hail of anti-aircraft fire enveloped them. The slow-moving and pilotless aircraft were easy to hit, but difficult to detonate from the ground. Half of the incoming V-1's, which travelled at a speed of about 370 miles per hour, were knocked out of the air by British Spitfires, which intercepted them as English radar picked them up.

By this time the destruction of the piers and warehouses at the West Indies dock was almost complete. The 2000-pound bombs were not selective. Civilian targets -- hotels, taverns, restaurants, schools and churches were virtually levelled or put out of existence, and nearly three thousand anti-combatants were killed during the time these death-dealing weapons were used. The English could only move as many women and children out of London as possible.

As the Allies advanced in France, they overran the Nazi V-1

launching sites, but the Germans had developed a new and deadlier version of the bomb, called a V-2. This weapon was faster than the speed of sound, and impossible to detect. It could also be directed by remote control, and launched from the Germans' top-secret base on Peenemünde Island, in the Baltic Sea.

Deadly as this weapon was, it came much too late in the war to affect the advance of the American, British and Canadian forces, after their landing on the beaches of Normandy.

Royal Air Force Liberator bombers pounded Peenemünde Island and destroyed the long landing fields that had been built to test the missiles. There was an unknown bonus to these attacks by the RAF -- the engine used in the V-2's, an early version of today's jet engine, was being modified by Hitler's technicians for installation in Hermann Göering's Luftwaffe fighters and bombers, and the runways were to be used for testing the new aircraft. Thus, jet fighters and bombers, which could conceivably have lengthened the war in Europe, were denied to the Nazis.

The attack was a brief one. When the all-clear sounded and Whitey and his pals came up out of their air-raid shelter, the devastation that greeted them was complete. Nothing remained of their barracks area. Why there were no flames or smoke was puzzling. Apparently the concussion of an exploding V-1 bomb had blown their living area apart. Clothes, bedding and papers were strewn about the remains of the building, and shards of glass from the structure's windows were imbedded in the few remaining wooden beams that still stood.

"Holy shit, guys," exclaimed Jonesy, a first class gunner's mate, "there ain't nothing left up here. All my clothes are blown to hell."

The tall, red-headed and freckled sailor shook his head in disbelief and wandered around, looking for something he could salvage from the mess.

Whitey stared at the pile of debris. He sat on a pile of rubble, in a state of shock.

CHAPTER 37

Whitey was assigned to the SS Samuel Morrison in September of 1944. The ship was actively engaged in running supplies from Liverpool to ports in Italy and southern France. The Morrison carried a complement of 20 Armed Guard sailors, with an experienced officer, Lieutenant O'Herlihy, as their CO.

Lieutenant O'Herlihy was a rare bird -- a Navy regular, who had actually graduated from Annapolis. No one knew why he'd been assigned to Armed Guard duty, but his crew was thankful to be working for him. O'Herlihy was a string-bean of a man, with a long nose and a thin face. He shambled, rather than walked, and his posture was stooped, as if he were ashamed of his six-foot-three frame. He treated his men fairly, and expected them to return the favor to him.

Many of the trips that the Morrison made ended in Livorno, or Leghorn, Italy, which is a port about fifty miles west of Florence, the beautiful Italian city of Renaissance buildings, art galleries and museums. Livorno, however, was a typical Italian seafaring city, and a big industrial center. To the sailors of the U.S. Navy, it was a good liberty port, and its bars, restaurants and whorehouses were always crowded during the years of World War II.

Whitey Houston and his shipmate Jonesy had taken the train from Livorno to the city of Pisa, home of the famous leaning tower. Neither was much impressed by the building.

"How long before this damn thing falls down, Whitey?" asked Jonesy. "Hell, these Eyetalians can't build any better than they can fight, looks to me."

"Back in school the teacher always raved about this place, but it doesn't look like much to me," said Whitey. "Let's get back to Leghorn and get drunk -- maybe we can pick up some of those good-looking Italian virgins."

The two caught the afternoon train back to Livorno and immediately headed for a bar down near the docks.

They had been drinking steadily for several hours and were half drunk, when a gang of noisy destroyer sailors burst into the bar and effectively took over the place.

A big husky bosun's mate came over to the end of the bar where Jonesy and Whitey were sitting and stood over them, eyeing them carefully.

"What tin can are you guys from?" he asked.

Whitey sensed that trouble was about to begin, but ignored the question.

Jonesy smiled up at the big sailor and said "Hell, man, we ain't from no destroyer. We're Armed Guard gunners from the SS Morrison."

"Well, shit, that's too bad, boys. This bar is tin can territory, as of right now. You can get your asses out of here, toot sweet," growled the bosun's mate.

Whitey's temper kicked in. He picked up his sturdy beer mug and brought it down on the big sailor's head, sending the man to the floor, but the huge bosun's mate was up quickly, grabbing Jonesy and flinging him across a row of stools at the bar.

Whitey grabbed one of the stools and swung it at the bosun's mate, slamming him against the railing of the bar. The man staggered back, then clutched his side and slipped to the floor. Whitey guessed he'd broken some ribs on the last maneuver. Out of the corner of his eye, he saw two of the big man's shipmates inching their way toward him. He threw the stool at them, sending them crashing into a nearby table, then grabbed Jonesy and helped him to his feet. He knew that the odds were seriously against him, but was ready to do as much damage as he could, while he could.

Suddenly, there was a blast of a whistle, and eight Shore Patrol sailors came running into the bar. The destroyer sailors ran for the exits. The Shore Patrol let them go. After all, their job was to maintain order, and order seemed to be back at the bar. Whitey, Jonesy and the big bosun's mate were the only ones left.

The SP officer strode into the bar, none other than Lieutenant O'Herlihy.

"What's happened here, men?" he asked.

"Sir, it looks like the bosun here had a few too many and fell off his bar stool. Looks like he hit his head when he fell. Isn't that right Boats?"

If looks could kill, Whitey would have been struck dead, but the big sailor knew when to keep his mouth shut. He nodded to the Lieutenant, but glared at Whitey.

"Boats," said Lieutenant O'Herlihy, "report to the fleet landing and go back to your ship. Have them look you over. Maybe you're hurt worse than it appears." He motioned one of the SP's over. "See that this man makes it back to the landing, sailor. It looks to me like he could use some help. Take him in the jeep, and take one other man with you, just in case."

The two SP's and the bosun's mate went out the door, and Lieutenant

O'Herlihy turned to Jonesy and Whitey.

"Houston and Jones -- I don't know what happened here, but I can guess. You've had too much to drink. Get the hell back to the Morrison, and try to stay out of trouble. Your liberty is cancelled as of right now. I'll talk to you tomorrow.

"Yes, sir" both men responded, then hurried out the door.

CHAPTER 38

In November of 1944 the Japanese were losing their battle to repulse American forces attacking Leyte. General MacArthur had established his headquarters on the eastern shore of that island in October, and Lex's ship, the SS Sharon Victory, was there, unloading munitions.

A kamikaze (Divine Wind) attack just the day before had caused the destruction of the SS Thomas Nelson. Three Armed Guard gunners and 240 Army personnel were reported killed, wounded, or missing.

Lex's gun crew had managed to shoot down one of the kamikaze attackers.

One of his shipmates said that an AG gunner aboard the SS Gus W. Darnell was blown overboard when the ship was torpedoed by a Japanese torpedo bomber. The man swam back to his ship, climbed up the anchor chain and then through the hawsepipe to the deck of the Darnell and returned to his gun station. Such was the valor, courage, dedication to duty and bravery of many of the Navy's Armed Guard crews.

These were dangerous days and the threat of the Japanese kamikaze pilots was constant. American Navy officers learned from the inspections of some of the downed kamikaze planes that they were provided gasoline for a one-way trip only. In some cases the cockpits of the planes were found to be sealed shut.

The Japanese sent a convoy with 8,000 troops, intended to reinforce their comrades on Leyte, but it was intercepted by the famous "Helldivers" from Admiral Halsey's Third Fleet, and destroyed.

Leyte fell to American forces the day before Christmas and the American forces celebrated the holiday and continued their island-hopping campaign in the Pacific.

The Captain of the SS Sharon Victory had donated four quarts of rum, and the cook of the ship mixed up a bowl of punch, using pineapple and apple juice, with raisins floating on top of the concoction. The merchant sailors and their shipmates, the Armed Guard gunners, toasted each other and observed the ending of the old year and the beginning of what might be the final days of the American campaign against the Japanese in the Pacific.

CHAPTER 39

Jeff Houston had been in the Navy for over two years and had finally made gunner's mate, third class. He was considered an outstanding petty officer by Lieutenant O'Keefe, his C.O. aboard the SS Wannamaker, an old WWI merchant vessel.

The war was winding down in Europe and Hitler's submarines were no longer the threat that they had been a year or two before, but they were still dangerous.

The Wannamaker was making a run between Trinidad and Boston, carrying a cargo of bauxite, the ore which is refined to obtain aluminum, and aluminum was in great demand during the second World War. The seas were calm and the crew of the ship were at ease. The men had celebrated the New Year of 1945 just a few days before.

Jeff and his shipmate, Harry Warren, a third class gunner's mate like himself, sat in the AG's quarters, in the stern of the Wannamaker, talking.

"Warren," said Jeff, "this damn war is going to be over soon -- at least in Europe. I don't think the japs will last much longer than the krauts. Hell, they couldn't handle us anyway and the Germans weren't much help to them in the Pacific."

"I don't know about that, Houston. War or no war, I'm staying in the Navy. There wasn't a hell of a lot of work back home anyhow. Remember how we used to say `I've found a home in the Navy?' Well, as far as I'm concerned, that's true. My father is a drunk and my mother never did have time for me and my sister, Becky. Becky's working in a factory back in Kansas. I think she's helping to put together bombers. Can you imagine? My little sister Becky. Shit!"

"All I want is to get out and get back to Catskill," said Jeff. "I haven't given any thought to what I'd be doing, but the Navy doesn't figure in it. Maybe I'll go to school and learn a trade. Or I could try to get on the Catskill Police. My older brother Jack was with them. When the war started he got a patriotic hair up his ass and went into the merchant marine. He was lost on the Alan Jackson, not too far from where we are right now. It was a tanker."

Warren shook his head. "Those babies go up like fire crackers, Houston. I'm lucky -- never got assigned to one."

The two men talked for another hour or so and then turned in for the night.

Captain Otto Werner, skipper of the U-953, had been waiting off Diamond Shoals, east of North Carolina's Cape Hatteras, for two days. He had observed the tempting target of the old freighter approaching and was ready when it passed.

One torpedo from the U-953 struck the bow of the Wannamaker and blew it off. A second deadly "fish" hit amidships and the ship disappeared in a tremendous explosion. There was no time for lifeboats to be launched. Wreckage was strewn over a two-mile area of the ocean.

The U-953 surfaced and headed east.

CHAPTER 40

The U.S. Tenth Army landed on the west coast of Okinawa on April Fools' day in 1945, in what was to be the last great amphibious operation of the war. At first, opposition was deceptively light, but then the Japanese fiercely and tenaciously resisted the invasion. American newspapers would later refer to this resistance as suicidal -- and the Japanese back home on their islands would talk of it as courageous. Such are the views of opposing sides in a war.

Lex's ship, the S.S. Burgoyne, had pulled into a deepwater harbor on the west coast of the island and anchored, awaiting its turn to offload the ship's massive cargo of gasoline and ammunition.

The crew was jumpy -- cargoes such as the Burgoyne carried always presented a hazard, even without the threat of Japanese submarines, and the gunnery crews were fully aware of the possibility of Japanese warplanes, operating out of airfields near the Okinawan town of Naha.

Lex thought with pleasure of his meeting with his brother Whitey, just two weeks before, in a temporary harbor off Iwo Jima. The fighting on that island had cost the U.S. Marines more than two thousand men, and the Japanese more than twenty thousand. Whitey was aboard the S.S. Jeremiah O'Brien, and the two ships had shared an anchorage, near each other. The two vessels exchanged movies, and their respective Armed Guard gun crews got together. Whitey and Lex were flabbergasted to meet each other, since neither knew the whereabouts of the other. Although each sailor occasionally wrote letters home, the mail was not reliable, and wartime censorship did not allow the identification of ships or their routes and locations.

Whitey was struck with Lex's new maturity. Gone was the idealistic bible-pounding youth of just three years ago. In his place was a bitter young man, who looked at life in a pessimistic way. Perhaps Will's death the previous year had hardened his outlook. Will had always been the baby brother, and now both the youngest and the oldest of the Houston boys were dead and gone, both as a result of the war.

"Lex," Whitey had said, "you've put on some weight, but you sure do look good to me. What do you hear from Fay Liston? I know mail is not too regular out here."

"Damn, Whitey, I can't tell you how good it is to see you. I had no idea where you were. The last I heard, you were somewhere in the north Atlantic, on that god-forsaken Murmansk Run, taking cargo to those Russkis."

Lex pointedly did not reply to Whitey's question about Fay Liston, so Whitey guessed that the romance was over.

"I feel pretty bad about missing Dad's funeral. Did you make it?"

Lex was visibly upset.

"No. My ship had already left port from the west coast. There was no way I could get home. Jeff didn't make it either, so Mom wrote. She's having a bad time, Whitey. First Jack, then Will, then Dad. She's losing everyone. I wonder if any of us will make it out of this thing."

"Cheer up Lex, we'll be in Tokyo before long. We've got those bastards on the run, finally. Things are looking up, believe me."

Lex lowered his head and seemed to be deep in thought.

"I got a letter from Mom, Whitey. She told me that Fay and Audrey are both dating other guys, probably a couple of draft dodging bastards. Fay never even had the decency to write and tell me that it was over. I don't know if Audrey has written to Jeff or not. Back in boot camp the Chaplain told us to be ready for "Dear John" letters, but none of us thought we'd get anything like that. All I know about Jeff is that he's in the Armed Guard, same as us, somewhere in the Atlantic. Sure hope he's not doing the Murmansk thing, like you did. Hell, wouldn't it be swell for us three to get together? Maybe we could tie one on -- have a high old time, for God's sake."

Whitey wasn't prepared to hear his brother talk like this. The war had been tough on Lex, and apparently his faith had not been strong enough to keep him from turning into a hard-hearted cynic.

"I got a note from Loretta, sometime around Christmas," said Whitey. "She's working in Jacksonville, at the shipyard -- welding. Can you imagine? Little Loretta with an acetylene torch."

Was it Whitey's imagination, or did Lex's face take on some color at the mention of Loretta?

The two brothers talked for several hours, until it was time for Whitey to return to the O'Brien. They shook hands, smiled at each other, and Whitey took the launch back to his ship.

The following day the O'Brien offloaded its cargo of jeeps and ammunition to a swarm of LCVP's. The ship left the harbor two days later. Lex thought it was headed back to America's west coast, to pick up another cargo, or perhaps it would stop in the Philippines and take on a load of soldiers and marines for the return trip to the States. He wondered when he'd be back in the U.S., and his hometown of Catskill, but he quickly put these thoughts out of his mind.

The harbor was filled with American warships, as well as many freighters, including both the Victory and the Liberty-type ships. Fighting raged on the southern tip of Okinawa and every American fighting man sensed that this battle might well be one of the most costly of the war.

Lex was standing on the deck of the Burgoyne when General Quarters sounded. He was wearing his lifejacket and helmet, so he quickly moved to his position at the gunmount and was joined in less than a minute by others of the gun crew. The alarm could mean only one thing here in the harbor -- air attack.

A single aircraft approached from the southeast, flying low on the horizon. The twenty-millimeter Oerlikon anti-aircraft guns opened up on the plane, which seemed to be flying much slower than the Japanese torpedo bombers or Zero fighters. Lex could not identify the plane from its silhouette.

The fusillade from the Burgoyne's guns, as well as a host of other AA's from the other ships in the harbor, seemed to envelop the tiny plane and a puff of smoke and a small finger of flame spurted from the aircraft's engine. But the plane continued in its flight, skimming just above the wavetops, and struck the Burgoyne at its stern, exploding in a brilliant flash of fire. The concussion of the blast blew several of the gun crew off their mount, into the water, where their lifeless bodies bobbed in the oil-slicked water.

Fire raged at the stern of the vessel, and the merchant seamen rushed back to put it out. Hoses were played over the blaze and for a moment it appeared that the worst was over.

The Burgoyne's first mate was directing the fire fighters and the ship's captain viewed the events from a position just outside the bridge, when a massive explosion erupted, vaporizing the men on deck and blowing the Burgoyne to bits.

Commander Weatherby, the skipper of a destroyer about a mile from the scene, witnessed the event, and the concussion of the blast threw him to the deck and broke glass on his bridge.

He knew that the airplane had been one of Japan's kamikaze craft, probably loaded with TNT, and that the merchant vessel's cargo of ammunition and gasoline had gone up as a result of the fire, but he could not spare time for sympathy for the men lost on the merchant vessel, for hundreds of Japanese dive bombers, torpedo planes and more kamikazes appeared over the horizon.

By the end of the battle for Okinawa on June 22, when American forces declared the territory secured, the Japanese had lost over 110,000 killed. Thousands of Japanese soldiers were sealed in their underground bunkers and left to die. The U.S. Navy and Naval Armed Guard gunners on merchant ships shot down 4,000 enemy planes. More than 3,000 kamikaze pilots flew their aircraft into American vessels, or the ocean, and were lost. two hundred vessels were hit and damaged and twelve American destroyers were sent to the bottom. Over twelve thousand sailors and marines were killed. Lex Houston was one of these statistics, but his brother Whitey would not know until months later.

The Okinawa battle was crucial to the winning of the war in the Pacific. The taking of the island gave the U.S. airfields to launch the swarms of big B29 "Flying Fortress" bombers which attacked the mainland of Japan, hitting Tokyo, Nagoya, Osaka and Kobe.

CHAPTER 41

There were many brothers, like the Houstons, who served in the armed services in World War II. The Lloyd brothers of North Carolina, three of whom were Naval Armed Guards, typify the patriotic spirit of these men.

May 5, 1945 found the SS Black Point, a 5300-ton collier, making a run from Boston to Galveston. bosun's mate sscond class Whitson Lloyd, one of the Armed Guard crew, stood on the stern enjoying the good weather.

His thoughts were serene and comfortable now. The war would soon be over, if he could believe the scuttlebutt he'd been hearing. He'd been a lucky sailor, for sure. Three years before, he'd been on his first merchant vessel, the SS Mormacdale. The ship steamed to Capetown, South Africa, then the Persian Gulf and finally Mozambique. The ship spent six days in a frightening typhoon, but survived the storm.

His second ship was the SS Expositor, which was in the first convoy to make the deadly Murmansk run. Twenty ships in the convoy were lost, but once again Lloyd's luck held. On the return voyage to the U.S., in 1943, the Expositor was hit by a torpedo. Its boilers exploded and the ship was sunk. Six merchant seamen and three armed guards lost their lives, but Lloyd, knocked unconscious and thrown into the water, was rescued by shipmates in one of the Expositor's lifeboats. Shortly after, the survivors were pulled from the water by HMCS Trillium and returned to shore at St. John's, Newfoundland.

After a short "R & R", Lloyd returned to duty aboard the SS Joseph P. Bradley, which made a run to the South Pacific. Again and again his ship avoided Japanese submarines, which were sinking ships ahead of them. And then it was the Persian Gulf again, with temperatures sometimes reaching 172 degrees. Men passed out from the heat each day, and the ship was hit by a fierce sand storm. The ship's food was nearly gone and the men were taking salt water showers.

The duty on the Bradley became a trip around the world, and Lloyd remarked in his diary "Five months and three days at sea out of seven and one-half months, 33,000 miles."

After returning to the U.S. he was assigned to another ship, the SS Eugene Hale, which steamed into the Mediterranean. He had been in Bari, Italy, shortly after the German attack, noting that there were thirty-six ships sunk in the harbor.

In November of 1944 Lloyd arrived aboard the SS Black Point, and had been aboard her ever since.

The war had been hard on him, but he did not regret it. That's why he'd enlisted in the first place -- to fight those German and Jap bastards who had attacked his country, and since then had claimed so many of his shipmates' lives.

He remembered his last home leave. The old hometown looked much the same as it had before he'd left. Most of his high school buddies had gone off to war, and some of them would not come back.

As he stood on the deck of his ship, he was unaware that the skipper of the German submarine U-853, Oberleutnant Frömsdorf, watched the Black Point from his periscope, several hundred yards away. Frömsdorf had received his orders from Admiral Dönitz that morning: "As from 5 May, 0800 hours cease fire x for U-boats at sea attacks forbidden x break off immediately pursuit of enemy."

Frömsdorf had no intention of ignoring this last prize. He ordered a torpedo fired at the ship. The result was deadly and immediate. The Black Point went down quickly.

The U-853 turned and ran, but the attack alerted several US Naval vessels which were in the vicinity. They pursued the U-853, which attempted to escape by lying on the bottom, noiseless.

U.S. sonar located the vessel, and depth charges were dropped until oil and debris indicated the submarine had been hit. Years later, divers located and explored the U-853, finding some of its torpedoes still in their tubes. The submarine became a tomb for Frömsdorf and his fifty-four crewmen.

But the young Armed Guard and eleven of his merchant marine shipmates were gone. Whitson Lloyd was the last Armed Guard killed in the Atlantic in World War II. His body was never found.

A few days later, "Victory In Europe" was proclaimed -- VE day.

CHAPTER 42

"**D**amn," said Filipowski, a third class gunner and Whitey's best friend, "This C-2 sure beats the hell out of our old Liberty ships."

Whitey and "Flip" had been aboard the S.S. Pampero, as AG gunners, since February of 1945, making runs from the west coast of the United States across the Pacific to Saipan, Tinian and Guam, all scenes of bloody battles with the Japanese in the previous three years.

But somehow, this trip looked like it would be different. In July, cargo was loaded at Port Chicago in California. There was nothing unusual about that, but suddenly all personnel boarding or leaving the ship were being checked closely by soldiers, and the ship was swarming with Army security officers.

Both men knew that Port Chicago, 30 miles northeast of San Francisco, had been the scene of a terrible munitions explosion, just one year before. More than 300 servicemen and civilians had been killed here, and almost 400 injured. The blast virtually levelled the nearby town of Port Chicago and broke windows fifteen miles away. It had been described by Naval officials as the most volatile man-made explosion in the history of the world and no one ever was able to come up with the cause. Was it an act of sabotage? No one knows, to this day.

Perhaps this was the reason Whitey and Filipowski were uneasy.

Special cargo, said to be "aerial mines," was stored in the aft hold. The hold was then sealed. The Army security people left, with the exception of Major Valley. Valley was an old man by Army standards, at thirty-six, although he appeared to be much younger. He was a career soldier, having been with the Army since 1927, and had risen through the ranks, finally receiving a battlefield commission in the Solomon Islands campaign, in 1942. Valley was big, tough, smart and dedicated.

The Pampero put to sea in the early morning hours of July fifth. The European war was over, but Japanese submarines, although generally not as effective as Admiral Dönitz' boats, still presented a serious threat. The merchant seamen were jumpy, for a number of reasons. Shipboard scuttlebutt had it that the ship would steam off the regular sea lanes -- at least 100 miles, if rumors were to be believed. To the utter amazement of the AG crew and their officer, Lieutenant Hager, the ship's port and starboard running lights blazed away into the night, with no explanation from the ship's master, Captain DeWar.

The AG lookouts sighted planes, all of them friendly, often during the ship's first two days at sea. They seemed to be keeping tabs on the Pampero.

Each day Major Valley checked the seals on the aft hold, once at daybreak and again at sunset.

The third day out, Lt. Hager met Major Valley coming from the ship's stern, and struck up a conversation.

"Major," said Hager, "have you got your sea legs yet?"

"Lt. Hager," laughed Valley, "I may have more sea time than you. I've crossed this pond five times so far, and was on a troop ship going to England before the Normandy invasion. I've gotta admit, though, when it gets rough, I stay topside all I can, otherwise my stomach gives me a problem."

"You've got me there, Major. I've only got a year's experience at sea, with the Armed Guard, and - thank the lord - never have been in any kind of battle. All I've ever done is gunnery practice. That suits me, though. I want this war to be over soon, and then I'm headed back to Ohio. My father runs a furniture store in Cleveland, and a job is waiting for me."

"Glad to hear it, Lieutenant. In a way I envy you. The Army is my career -- that's all I've ever known. When peace comes, I guess I'll find myself at some Army base back in the states, pushing a pencil -- at least for a couple of years, and then I can retire. But I'll probably stay for thirty. I don't know much else than the Army. Hell, the Army is the reason my wife left me."

"Say, Major," asked Lt. Hager, "what do we have stored back aft that's so damned secret?"

Major Valley's face darkened, his lips tightened, and his huge frame tensed. He seemed ready to attack the young Lieutenant, then quickly relaxed and looked away for a moment.

"Lieutenant Hager," said Valley, "this ship is depending on your crew, in case we run into any trouble. This cargo is important -- very important. But aside from that -- what we're carrying is none of your damned business right now. Don't ask me again."

With that, the Major quickly turned and walked forward. Lieutenant Hager knew he'd made a mistake.

Unknown to the men aboard the Pampero, the U.S.S. Indianapolis was also on its way to Tinian, also carrying what the crew were told was "aerial bombs."' The Indianapolis did not carry any anti-submarine gear, since it depended solely on its speed to evade submarines. It made the run from the Farallons (a group of seven rocky islands, 30 miles off the coast of California) to Diamond Head, Hawaii, a distance of 2,091 miles, in 74-1/2 hours on the outbound leg of its journey to Tinian.

The War Department was taking no chances. There is no record of other ships carrying parts of "`aerial bombs,'" but in August of 1945 several atomic bombs were assembled at Tinian and the air strip there was used by the planes that dropped these weapons of death and destruction on Japan.

On its return trip to the United States, in July of that year, the Indianapolis was sunk by the Japanese submarine I-58. The Navy did not know of the sinking for several days, and many hundred sailors perished, either by drowning or shark attacks, while they floated amongst the debris of their sunken ship. The commander, Captain Charles McVay, was the only commanding officer in U.S. Navy history to be court-martialled for the loss of his ship in wartime. Some years later Captain McVay committed suicide.

CHAPTER 43

The furious and costly battle for Okinawa convinced President Harry Truman and his military advisers that an invasion of the mainland of Japan would exact a cost beyond comprehension. Despite the destructive fury of American B-29 bombers with their raids on the cities of Tokyo, Nagoya, Osaka and Kobe, along with many other military targets, the resolve of the Japanese military showed no signs of flagging.

A Presidential commission of scientists and other authorities had recommended to President Truman that he use the newly-developed atomic bomb on Japan, to avoid a costly and time-consuming invasion. Others in the U.S. argued against its use. These people argued that Japan should be forewarned of what was to be done to them, even to the point of dropping it on some unoccupied area.

President Truman made the decision to drop the bomb. The parts of the weapon were put aboard ships and sent to the tiny island of Tinian, where they were assembled. On August 6, 1945, the first wartime nuclear weapon was used, on the city of Hiroshima. It had more power than 20,000 tons of TNT, better than two thousand times the power of the largest bomb ever dropped before.

At Hiroshima, the conditions were just right for the creation of a huge firestorm. The heat of the fire caused an intense updraft, producing strong winds, which were drawn toward the center of the burning area. Those winds fanned the flames and converted the area into a holocaust. Everything which could burn, did burn.

Sixty percent of the entire city was destroyed. An estimated 130,000 people were killed, injured or missing, and the number which died later of wounds, burns, shock and radiation, is unknown.

The Allies received no reply to their demand for unconditional surrender by the Japanese. The Japanese will to fight still was strong, and the Imperial military command was making plans to draft millions of women and children into a "home defense" force.

The decision was made to drop a second bomb, and this was done on the city of Nagasaki, on August ninth. The destruction of this second bomb rivalled that of the first.

On August tenth. Emperor Hirohito exerted his influence on the military commanders and the Japanese surrendered.

CHAPTER 44

The date was September 2, 1945.

The U.S. Fleet had been in Tokyo harbor since the twenty-ninth of August and the battleship U.S.S. Missouri was among the mighty warships there. Tokyo bay was shrouded by gray and threatening clouds.

A group of Japanese officials, headed by the Japanese foreign minister, Mamoru Shigemitsu, boarded the ship to sign the official unconditional surrender. Shigemitsu limped as he came aboard, favoring his artificial wooden leg, the result of an assassination attempt by a Korean national in Shanghai, years before. He would be one of the signers of the surrender, but did not know that he would later be convicted of war crimes and sent to prison for seven years.

Days before, Emperor Hirohito had issued a proclamation instructing his subjects to cease hostilities, lay down their arms, and carry out the terms of the surrender. Japanese soldiers in China, Formosa, Manchuria and many of the islands in the Pacific surrendered to Allied commanders, and World War II was over. Some of Japan's troops, stationed in out-of-the-way jungles and deserted islands, either did not "get the word," or chose not to honor it. As much as twenty-five years later, Japanese troops would continue to straggle back to civilization, but this day would go down in history as "VJ" day, for `Victory in Japan.'

Whitey watched the ceremony from the top of a gun turret. He had been sent to the Missouri with a case of champagne for Admiral Halsey, and delivered it to the ship's Chief Storekeeper, then stayed for a cup of coffee. The skipper of his Merchant Vessel, Captain Van Rensellaer, thought it might be a nice gesture on his part, due to the gravity of the day. Whitey's CO, Lieutenant Vollmer, agreed and picked Whitey for the delivery.

"Houston, why not hang around for the festivities?" asked the chief. "They won't miss you back on that rust bucket you came from."

Whitey knew the chief was right and he was soon lost in the crowd aboard the massive battleship. Even though he was only twenty years old, Whitey knew full well that he was witnessing one of the most dramatic moments in American history. Whitey's CO aboard the merchant vessel said he thought it ironic that the Missouri had been Halsey's first duty assignment, when he'd graduated from the Naval Academy, years before.

Just as the historic document was signed, and the twenty-minute ceremony ended, the sun burst through the clouds.

General MacArthur stepped to a microphone rigged on deck, and said "It is my earnest hope and indeed the hope of all mankind, that from this solemn occasion a better world shall emerge out of the blood and carnage of the past."

One thing for sure, thought Whitey, he had to make plans for his future now that the war was over. He was very uncertain of what he would do.

CHAPTER 45

It was late in the day and the snow lay deep and drifted on the roads in and around Catskill, when the Greyhound bus dropped Whitey off in front of his mother's home, just outside of town. The bus normally dropped all of its passengers at the terminal in town, but the driver made an exception in Whitey's case. After all, he was in uniform and in those days a man in uniform was respected. The driver asked Whitey where he lived and then drove there.

It was a week before Christmas, in 1945, and Whitey had decided to take some leave from his duty station, the Armed Guard Center in New Orleans.

As he walked up the driveway, the front door of the house was flung open and Mrs. Houston hurried out to the porch to meet him.

"Whitey, Whitey, oh my god, it's been so long. Why didn't you call?"

"Hi mom -- I'm sorry -- I couldn't get near a phone. It's so close to the holidays and a lot of the guys are headed home and getting mustered out. I paid a guy to get his bus ticket -- he was going to Albany. You can't get a bus or train ticket anywhere. But I wanted to come home."

The bus ride through town had brought back a lot of old recollections, but at the same time it gave him the feeling of entering a foreign country, although little of the scenery had really changed in the three years he'd been gone.

He and his mother sat up until well past midnight and talked, drinking cup after cup of Mrs. Houston's strong coffee. In the early hours of the morning, Whitey said good night to his mother and went up the stairs to his old bedroom. The room was clean, as it should have been, since Mrs. Houston swept and dusted it each week, even changing the sheets on the bed. In the back of her mind she'd always known Whitey would be back, although his infrequent cards and letters never mentioned his plans. She knew her son's unpredictability well.

Whitey had his breakfast at Aggie's the morning after his arrival home. Teddy Kolokotrones was in a rest home, after suffering a serious stroke in the spring of 1945 and Ruthie Weiss, now the wife of Phil

Harrison, the new police chief of Catskill, had bought the restaurant. It was not the same place without the jolly little Greek, but most of the early risers in Catskill still met there.

Whitey was saddened as he thought of his mother's apparent decline in health. From a big and commanding woman she had seemed to shrink -- or perhaps this was just his view of her. He knew she had suffered blow after blow in the last three years, with scarcely any time to recover from any of them. First Jack, then Will, her husband, and finally Jeff and Lex.

She'd told him that she no longer was the church organist and choir director, and seldom attended church. Whitey knew better than to carry this discussion any further because he knew it would inevitably lead to a discussion of her former strong faith, and his mother did not seem anxious to elaborate.

Mona Bell, Will's old girl friend, was now a waitress at Aggie's and she had put on a lot of weight.

"Whitey -- golly, I haven't seen you in a long time. You're looking like a million bucks. Are you back for good?"

"Hello Mona, you don't look so bad yourself. No - hell, I don't know. I've got a few days of leave and this is my first time home in a long while. What are the Liston girls doing?"

"My lord, Whitey. Didn't you hear? Oh gosh - they were both killed in a car crash last winter. Audrey and Fay were out with two fellows from Kingston. They were coming home late and the car slid on some ice -- at least that's what the State Troopers think. Anyway, it turned over in a creek. All four of them were trapped inside and drowned. The car must have smashed through the ice in the creek. They weren't even found until the next morning. It was just horrible, Whitey, just horrible."

He could see that Mona was upset, and she turned her head away and wiped a tear with a corner of her apron.

There was a time when this kind of news would have shocked him, but too many of his shipmates and friends - and his own brothers, had been killed in the war. Some of his shipmates had been alongside him when they died. The experience had hardened him in some ways, softened him in others, and had made him more appreciative of his own life.

"Mona, get me a western omelette and a cup of coffee, please."

"Sure Whitey. If you need anything else, anything at all, just let me know."

As she turned to go back to the kitchen, she winked at Whitey. For some reason, this struck him as funny, and he laughed out loud.

Mona brought his breakfast soon after, and as Whitey ate, he was deep in thought. He was twenty, and the only job he'd ever had was shooting cannons and anti aircraft guns, aboard U.S. Merchant ships -- hardly a good recommendation for any civilian position. But he was top man in his rate, and had made second class gunner's mate, fast advancement for the Navy in those days. His personnel officer at the AG Center was encouraging him to stay in. The Navy needed people, especially now that most GI's were getting out, flocking to their old and new jobs and entering college on the GI Bill. In his heart Whitey knew that he would have a difficult time as a civilian.

"Houston," his personnel officer had said, "so many good people are mustering out that we're getting short-handed. And we still need experienced men to man our ships. There's a lot of work to be done in Europe, and the Navy will be in the thick of things, running supplies over there. The Army will probably have the biggest job, what with the military occupation and working with the new governments, but they'll need supplies, and a lot of manpower will be going back and forth. That means we've still got plenty of work to do, and we'll need help."

Whitey finished his coffee and, true to his unpredictable nature, in the next moment decided to leave Catskill a day or two early and spend some time in Jacksonville, Florida. Jack's wife Loretta was there with her two daughters, and she was the last remaining member of he and his brothers' group. He wanted very much to see her. Why, he did not really know. First thing in the morning, he'd try to get a bus or train ticket to Florida. Hell, if it came to that, he'd start hitchhiking, one or the other.

CHAPTER 46

He hitchhiked from New York to Philadelphia, wearing his Naval uniform, since it was a sure key to getting a ride, and spent the night in a YMCA there. In the morning, he talked himself into a ride with a long haul trucker he'd met in a diner near the Y. The trucker was headed for Atlanta, and Whitey rode with him as far as Richmond, Virginia. His luck continued and he was able to get a ticket for the overnight train to Jacksonville. On the train, he slept like a dead man, and woke up Saturday morning as the train pulled into the station in Florida.

Amazingly, he found Loretta's name and address in a phone book at the station, and called her home. As far as he knew, Loretta had not remarried. Her job at the shipyard and raising two girls alone must have been a demanding challenge and he guessed she hadn't had much of a social life. The phone rang for only a few moments, then a young voice answered.

"Hello," said Whitey. "Who is this?"

"This is Donna Houston," said the voice.

"Donna, this is your Uncle Whitey."

There was a long hesitation, then a cry of delight.

"Uncle Whitey! Gee -- I can't believe it. Are you calling from Catskill? How is Grandma Houston?"

"No, Donna. I'm at the train station here in Jacksonville. Grandma is fine. My train just got in."

Whitey could hear shouting in the background. Donna was relaying the information to someone else -- perhaps her sister Karen, or her mother. There was the sound of the telephone being dropped, and then silence. He thought for a moment he'd been disconnected.

"Whitey," said the familiar voice of Loretta Houston, "Is it really you? And are you really here in Jacksonville?"

"You bet, Loretta. I got into town about a half hour ago. I had a short visit with mom. I've still got a few days' leave left before I have to be back in New Orleans and I really wanted to see you and the kids. Thanks for writing to me all those times. It cheered me up to get word from home, and you and Mom Houston were the only ones that ever dropped me a line."

Loretta laughed the musical, exciting laugh that he remembered.

When he was fifteen, he thought he was in love with her. He'd felt guilty about those thoughts at the time. He'd had no reason or right to think them. She was married to his brother, a brother that he idolized.

"You won't recognize the kids, Whitey. They're not such kids anymore. Donna is going steady -- I really think she's too young, but times have changed since the war ended, I guess. Will you come and have supper with us, and stay awhile? You can use the couch in our living room. The house isn't very big, but you'll be comfortable."

The taxi dropped Whitey off at Loretta's house, a small bungalow on the outskirts of Jacksonville, in a somewhat shabby neighborhood. The cabbie, an older man, refused to be paid.

"Good luck to you, sailor," the man called to him as he drove away.

Whitey saw a small flag with a gold star fastened to the cab's rear window, indicating the driver had lost someone in the war. A lot of the windows in Jacksonville displayed them as well, since this was a Navy town.

Donna and Karen ran down the walk to meet him. He was stunned at how much the girls had grown, and how beautiful they both were, and it made him feel much older than his twenty years. Donna was the mirror image of her mother -- short, pert and blonde, with a striking figure, and Karen had an unmistakable and eerie resemblance to his late brother, Jack. A sudden feeling of sorrow struck him, but he managed to put it out of his mind. Karen was tall for her age, a thin girl, blessed with jet-black hair and friendly brown eyes. Whitey had been the girls' favorite uncle, and he'd always treated them like his sisters. Hell, thought Whitey, he wasn't much older than they were.

Loretta stood in the doorway, smiling. She was still a beautiful woman, but the loss of her husband had aged her, lines were etched around her eyes and she seemed to be a much more mature woman now than when Whitey had last seen her. He caught a hint of sadness in her smile.

Loretta threw open her arms, then held and hugged him. Tears ran down her cheeks and he was embarrassed.

Was it his imagination, or did she hold him just a little longer than necessary? Secretly, Whitey was pleased.

Supper was the best meal Whitey had eaten in months, and he knew he was getting the VIP treatment.

Loretta said that her job at the shipyard was winding down and that she'd been going to hairdresser's school at night. It was plain to her that many of the jobs previously open to women would now be filled by returning GIs. Whitey recognized Loretta's sharp mind at work here. She'd looked at the situation and made her plans. He knew she was a survivor and a tough woman, in some ways stronger than his mother.

He told her of his plans to make the Navy a career and she nodded, agreeing that he probably was making the right choice.

"Whitey, you've grown up a lot since you enlisted. The Navy has been good for you. I hope you won't mind me saying this -- but you were headed for trouble before you went in. We all knew that, and so did you."

She was right, he thought, and he nodded in response.

Donna and Karen cleared the table, then brought two cups of coffee, and disappeared.

"You've got them trained pretty well, Loretta," said Whitey.

"Not really," said Loretta. "They're good kids. They usually do the right thing. Jack was strong in that department, and kids pay more attention to their parents than most people realize. He was a good example for them."

"Donna wants to call her boy friend. They may be going to a movie tonight and Karen and two of her friends are going roller skating at the rink. It's just around the corner. They knew we'll be talking grownup talk, and teenagers aren't interested in that."

Whitey was a little uncomfortable. He wasn't good at small talk, and being around Loretta made him nervous. He came from a different world, a world of killing and dying and fighting the sea. A world where men on leave got drunk, fought with each other, and crowded into the bars and bordellos at their ports of call. Civilians didn't understand his kind and he had to admit that he didn't understand them either. Hell, he'd never really been one, one of those nine to five people who brought home a paycheck every week, and took a one or two-week vacation every year with their families.

Loretta seemed to sense his discomfort. She reached across the table and covered his hand with hers. It was as if she somehow understood him and was trying to make him comfortable.

But the act had the opposite effect. It caused the blood to rush to his head and he found that he was suddenly short on conversation. Loretta looked into his eyes and he returned her look, but found himself unable to think clearly. He would have stayed that way, but Loretta abruptly removed her hand and spoke.

"I've never told this to a soul, Whitey, but I've got to tell you. It's been bothering me for years. Right after Jack joined the Merchant Marine -- we'd had a terrible fight about that, and I threatened to leave him. I think he knew I'd never do that, but his mind was made up. He was such a brave man, and patriotic. I know it sounds corny, but that's exactly the kind of person he was. I was angry with him, and missed him terribly -- and then, partly to get even with him, and maybe because I just couldn't help myself, I seduced Lex."

There was a long silence and she lowered her eyes in embarrassment.

Whitey couldn't believe his ears, but he remembered Lex's reaction back in Iwo Jima, earlier in the year, when he'd mentioned hearing from Loretta. He felt certain that she was telling the truth.

"I knew I'd done something very wrong," she continued, "against my upbringing and everything my mother had taught me, but felt it was a kind of revenge for what Jack had done to me and the girls. I made excuses -- I was so lonely, and Lex was so sympathetic -- and desirable. Then Jack was killed, and I was convinced that God was punishing me for my sins. Later, when Lex was killed, I was certain that we were all being punished. But now that I've had time to think about it, I don't believe any of that. I'm just a human being, like everyone else, and what I did with Lex happened in a moment of weakness. It's water under the bridge, and worrying about why it happened doesn't do anyone any good. Do you hate me for that, Whitey? Can you understand why it happened?"

He never expected to be put into a situation like this.

"Lex never said a word about it, Loretta. You and I are the only ones that know, unless you've told your mother or Mom Houston. You're right -- it's water under the bridge. None of us can change anything now, and I think I know how you felt back then. Do you think you're the only one that this has happened to? Hell, I've talked to guys on some of my ships who never missed a chance to cheat on their wives, and they told me their wives were doing the same thing back home. The war has put everyone through the wringer, Loretta. But you're still alive and have two great girls to raise. It seems to me that you've done a damn fine job so far. Jack would be proud of you for that."

"Whitey," said Loretta, "Before you went into the Navy, everyone said you'd never amount to anything, the way you drank and gambled. But they were wrong. I think Jack would be pleased with the way you turned out. You know that he always thought a lot of you. I feel better now that we've talked."

He looked into her eyes, and saw the sadness and regret reflected there. His heart softened toward her and he felt a mixture of sympathy and love for this beautiful woman.

Loretta got up from her chair, stared at him for a moment,   as if she were trying to make a decision. She came around the table, leaned down, and kissed him squarely on the lips. The kiss was a long and passionate one. Whitey stood up and drew her to him, returning her kiss with one of his own. His mind raced and his heart pounded.

"Whitey, when the girls leave, I want you to come to bed with me," said Loretta.

CHAPTER 47

Early in January, he received word that he'd been promoted to first class gunner's mate, and received his orders for Norfolk, Virginia. He was to report there by the end of the month. He'd been assigned to the U.S.S. Nantahala, a fleet oiler. He had no idea what his duties would be aboard this huge ship, but it wasn't a combat vessel, and he was a gunnery specialist. He was told that it would be leaving for a Mediterranean cruise in March.

In the meantime, Whitey thought long and hard about his visit with Loretta. It had been the most natural thing in the world for him to go to bed with her, and he'd shared her bedroom each night that he stayed at her home. He would make his bed on her couch in the living room, then go to her room after the girls had gone to sleep. He suspected that Loretta's daughters knew what was going on, but they gave no sign of it.

He felt no guilt now. After all, Loretta was a widow. Whitey had been out in the world for a few years, and even though he had just turned twenty-one, was well experienced in the area of feminine relationships, even though most of those relationships involved payment afterwards. It was the way of seafarers the world over.

There was a nagging feeling in his mind about what the future would hold for him and Loretta. Hell, she was nearly thirty-two, eleven years older than he. And what about the two girls?

He put everything out of his mind, as young men sometimes do, thinking that things would take of themselves.

The Personnel office gave Whitey train tickets for Norfolk. He packed his seabag, then picked up his records and a copy of his orders. His train was due to leave early the next morning. He went to a pay booth and called his mother in Catskill.

"Hi mom," he said. "This is Whitey. I've got my orders for Norfolk, Virginia. I'll be picking up my ship there, and then we'll be sailing for

Europe and the Mediterranean sometime in March."

"I missed you over Christmas, Whitey. I spent the holidays with my sister in Kingston. When will you be coming home again?"

"I doubt if I can get any leave between now and when my ship goes to the Med. We'll be over there at least four months, maybe longer, with the 6th Fleet. When I get back, I'll come on up to Catskill. That will most likely be in September, though, mom."

"Whitey, you take care of yourself. You're all I've got now."

He hung up the phone and placed a call to Loretta.

The phone rang just once, then was quickly answered by Loretta.

"Loretta -- this is Whitey. I've got my orders and I leave in the morning for Norfolk. I wanted you to know. I'm sorry I haven't called you before this, but there's been a lot to do here in the Armed Guard Center. They're re-assigning everyone. No need to have the AG's any more, I guess."

There was a long silence on the other end and Whitey wondered if they'd been disconnected. He was startled when Loretta spoke.

"Whitey. I feel bad about having to tell you this. I'm pregnant."

CHAPTER 48

There had never been any question in Whitey's mind that he would marry Loretta, after she told him of the pregnancy, but she surprised him. When he proposed, she at first refused, saying that she needed some time to think.

Whitey waited two weeks and then called her.

She was in tears.

"Whitey, I don't want you to think I'm trapping you. When you walked into my life again last Christmas, my heart almost stopped. There hasn't been anyone in my world since Jack died and I thought I'd never feel about anyone the way I felt about him. But I was wrong. The chemistry, or whatever you want to call it -- the spark, the electricity when I touch you. I can't deny it. But you're only a young man -- if you want to back out of this, I won't blame you."

"Loretta -- I guess I was always envious of Jack. He deserved you. He was the best man I've ever known. I never dreamed I had a chance with you. Please marry me. I'll be a good father to our baby and I'll take care of Donna and Karen like Jack would have, if he'd lived."

Loretta sobbed for a full minute. Then, she collected herself and said yes.

The wedding took place in late February in Jacksonville, at the Methodist church Loretta and her two girls attended. Mrs. Houston came down from Catskill on the train and Loretta's mother sat with her in the church. Donna and Karen were bridesmaids and Chief DiNardi, one of Whitey's Armed Guard shipmates who was also assigned to the Nantahala, acted as his best man.

Whitey had asked DiNardi just a week before the wedding and was surprised when he agreed. Whitey thought of this in later years -- hell, he didn't make friends easily -- he was a loner. But DiNardi had been raised in an orphanage in Philadelphia, and was a loner too. Their friendship would last for many years.

Whitey wondered what his mother thought of the marriage. Did she resent Whitey's marrying a woman eleven years his senior? He need not have worried on this account. Emma Houston had not seen much of her grandchildren since they'd moved to Florida, and she loved them with all her heart. Loretta and Mrs. Houston recognized each other's strengths and weaknesses, and now that Loretta was "back in the family," again, Mrs. Houston felt restored in some small way to the status of grandmother. She felt that she'd be seeing a lot of the girls from now on. And Loretta's mother was delighted to have her daughter married once more, even to a much younger person, though she still had some reservations about the wild and immature Whitey Houston. Neither of the mothers knew that Loretta was expecting, and if they had, they would both have been delighted at the prospect of a new grandchild.

The Nantahala stayed with the Sixth Fleet longer than expected, closing out six months on station in the Mediterranean, refueling the ships of the fleet.

Loretta and the girls remained in Jacksonville.

Just before the oiler was scheduled to return to Norfolk, the Red cross notified Whitey that he was the father of a healthy nine-pound baby boy. Loretta and Whitey had agreed to name him Jack, after Whitey's late older brother.

Nothing can bring home the sense of responsibility to a young husband more than the birth of a son or daughter. Whitey bought two boxes of cigars and handed them out to his crewmates on the Nantahala. His initial sense of elation was replaced by sobering thoughts of the future, and how the new addition to his family would change his life.

CHAPTER 49

-March 1951-

The last five years had been hectic. After the end of World War II, another conflict started -- this one called the "Cold War." Hatred and emotions ran high, and some of America and Britain's allies of the last war were now enemies. Conversely, some of their enemies were now close partners in trade.

Nationalism was running wild in France, and now that country was decidedly cool to the United States. The Union of Soviet Socialist Republics was calling in its markers all over the world and the tentacles of Communism reached everywhere, including American Universities and the government. Senator Joe McCarthy had stirred up the country, claiming communists were under every bed, and conducted a series of "witch hunts'" blacklisting anyone who was suspected of having any left-wing beliefs.

In 1950, North Korea invaded South Korea. Seoul, the capital of the country, fell quickly to the communists. The new United Nations organization decided to intervene, and General MacArthur was given command of the United Nations forces in South Korea.

The National Guard, Marines, Army and Navy were all mobilized, and the draft once more went into effect. By October of 1950, the Chinese Communists had entered the war. By March of 1951, however, the Chinese had been driven out of Korea, as a result of the superior firepower and airpower of the American troops.

Whitey had been stationed in San Diego and Loretta and his son Jack were living there too. Donna was married to a sailor from Jacksonville and was now living in Norfolk, while her husband was with the Sixth Fleet in the Mediterranean. Karen was engaged to a high school teacher, and still lived back in Jacksonville. She was attending business school at night, and working days as a secretary in a Real Estate office.

Whitey was now a Chief Gunner's Mate. He'd been assigned to the U.S.S. Missouri and took part in the bombarding of Korea before he was suddenly reassigned to Bainbridge, Maryland.

He took the Pullman train to Baltimore from San Diego, a trip of five days, then a bus to the Naval Training Center, where he was to meet with his new boss, Commander Kennedy.

"Chief Houston, welcome to the Naval Training Center," said Commander Kennedy, seated behind the grey Navy issue desk in his new office, located in the refurbished administration building of the Naval Training Center.

"We've just re-opened the Training Center in March," he said. "As you know, I'm the Exec here. The center was de-activated back in June of 1947. Last year, the Navy Department decided that we needed more facilities for training boots, so here we go again."

"I was a gunnery officer myself -- and I see by your record that you've been in the Armed Guard. A good group of men, Chief. They had the shit blown out of them in WWII. I know that. I was aboard the USS Willis. We were part of an anti-submarine Killer group in the Atlantic. We got eight subs while I was on the Willis, and I'm proud of that. We need people like yourself, Chief, to train these snot-nosed kids they're sending us now. Who knows, maybe we're in for another big war -- not that the Korean thing isn't bad enough, even though the papers call it a `police action.' Shit, you can get killed just as dead!"

"Yes, sir," replied Whitey, "Training boots will be something new for me. I took my boot training here myself, back in October of 1942."

"We'll set you up for training, Chief Houston. You'll act as an assistant company commander. There'll be an experienced chief working as the company commander, and you'll learn the ropes that way. While you're learning, we'll want you to teach some gunnery classes to the boots. Lieutenant Coffee will see that you get established here, and help you get your family moved from San Diego. You're assigned to the First Regiment area. We have three regiments of male boots. The Fourth Regiment has the only WAVE recruit training school in the Navy. We expect to have 4500 young women training there before we're through. Good luck, Chief."

"Thank you, sir," said Whitey.

CHAPTER 50

-1952-

Whitey had trained six companies of recruits and he believed that he was doing something right. Four of those companies had been named "Hall of Fame," a boot-camp designation which spotlighted outstanding companies -- those which had earned high marks in marching, scholarship, athletics and leadership. The companies which stood out among their peers were awarded flags, one for each specialty. Those few groups with a large number of flags were designated "Hall of Fame," which earned them special privileges. This was one of the highest honors which could be bestowed by the Naval Training Center. Whitey's last company had been given a Naval Training Center Citation, the very pinnacle of recognition at the Training Center.

Just like anyone who is doing a good job, and receiving recognition for it, Whitey felt great pride in his work. This was likely the reason that he began to spend so much time at the Bainbridge Chief's Club. He enjoyed the praise of his fellow chiefs and the club gave him an outlet from the stress of pushing recruits to their limits. At first, his drinking consisted of three or four beers at the end of the day. Then, he began to add a few whiskey chasers. Finally, four or five beers with chasers began to be the order of the day, and he held to this regimen for several months. His work began to deteriorate, although his fellow chiefs held their comments to themselves. They knew Whitey's temper could be an awesome thing indeed.

One night he came home at midnight, staggering drunk. Loretta, who had been keenly aware of his drinking and could see that it was becoming a problem, both for Whitey and herself and little Jack, tried to talk to him, but he would not listen. Just before he passed out on the rug of their rented apartment, he'd thrown a frying pan through the screen of their new TV set. Luckily, their small son was sound asleep in the bedroom and didn't hear the noise.

Somehow, Whitey was able to get to work the next morning. Loretta called the personnel office at the base and made an appointment to talk to Lieutenant Wagner, the woman who ran the alcohol abuse program. Lt. Wagner was a very busy woman in 1952.

Loretta arrived at Lt. Wagner's office at ten. Jack was in school and she took a taxi from their apartment to the base.

"Mrs. Houston," said Lt. Wagner, "call me Joan. This is a woman to woman discussion."

"Joan -- I feel uncomfortable calling a Naval officer by her first name," said Loretta. "But I'm worried about my husband. He's a good man but lately he's been getting irritable. He doesn't sleep well, and he comes home smelling like he's tried to clean out all the stock at the Chief's Club."

"Mrs. Houston -- hell, Loretta, let's drop the formalities. I can appreciate your concern. I know what you're going through. My first husband was an alcoholic. He was a Lieutenant Commander, and I was an ensign in the nurse corps. He wouldn't admit to his problem. But one night in Wahiawa -- we were stationed in Hawaii then -- he went off the road and over a cliff in his car. It burned. End of story. I got out of the medical end and went into personnel. The Navy thinks they can help some of their people before it's too late -- and the other services are starting to work on the problem."

"I don't want him to get into trouble, Joan. He's always been a fairly heavy drinker, but seemed able to handle it. But he's been under a lot of pressure lately. He's pushed six companies of boots through training in the last fifteen months. He talks about his problem "kids," as he calls them, all through the training period. And last month he told me he'd thrown "some punk" off the second floor fire escape of one of the barracks. He said the kid was giving him headaches. The kid was scared -- he got a broken arm, but he told the sick bay that he'd fallen while he was horsing around with another boot. Can you help us?"

"Loretta, if you can get him to come in to the sick bay, we'll have one of the psychologists talk to him. Alcoholics can be identified in a lot of ways, and the Navy can help them. On the other hand, from what you've told me, if your husband doesn't get some kind of help, and soon, the Navy may have to give him the boot. He's got ten years in, right? I've pulled his record. He's got a good reputation and we wouldn't want to lose him. I'll leave it up to you and your husband. If he'll cooperate, fine. If not, then it may be just a matter of time before he gets into some really hot water. So far, his record doesn't have anything bad on it, so the Navy isn't about to do anything, and without some justification, it all ends right here. I'm glad you came in to talk with me. Our conversation won't go out of this room. Use whatever influence you have, Loretta, and get your husband to ask for some help."

Loretta felt she had found a friend, someone who had been through more trouble than she, and someone who had given her some valuable advice.

CHAPTER 51

Lieutenant Wagner had not been entirely truthful with Loretta. Soon after Loretta Houston left her office, she made some telephone calls.

A few days later Whitey was asked to report to the medical department, for some psychological testing. He was a little confused about this. After ten years in the navy, he thought they knew just about everything about him. But maybe they had some kind of new job that required a test to qualify for. What the hell, he thought, I've got the time. What do I have to lose?

Lieutenant Wagner called Whitey in to her office, and told him to sit down.

"Chief Houston, I'll get right down to business. We've had you answer some questions and run you through a series of tests. We've also talked to some of your shipmates and the bartenders over at the Chief's club. The Navy's done enough work in this area to be certain that we know what we're doing here."

"Lieutenant Wagner, I don't know what's going on."

"Chief, you're an alcoholic -- don't bother to tell me you're not. We've got enough information on you to know better. There was a time when we'd toss you out of the service, but things have changed. I'll put it very simply -- either you sign up for the alcoholic treatment program or you're out."

Whitey Houston didn't bother to argue the point. He knew full well that the Lieutenant was probably right. He'd been hitting the booze pretty heavy lately and it had begun to affect his work. Hell, that kid he threw off the fire escape -- he felt bad about that. The kid had just been messing his whole company up, and it was reflecting on Whitey's leadership. Normally, he'd have chewed the kid out, but this time the young sailor gave him some lip. Whitey lost his head on that one, he knew. There was only one path he could take, if he wanted to stay in the Navy, and he wanted to stay, that was certain. It was the only life he'd known, and he didn't want to start over in something else. So, he signed the papers the Lieutenant put in front of him.

The U.S. Navy had been operating what would today be called a "Betty Ford" type of clinic, in Jacksonville, Florida, for several years. They recognized the value of their investment in the training of their more senior people, and knew that alcoholism was beginning to be a major problem for all the armed forces.

Whitey spent six months in the program.

Loretta had moved with little Jack to Jacksonville, and put him in the school system there. She took a job as a hair dresser in a beauty salon.

Jack was home with a baby-sitter and Whitey and Loretta were having a late supper at a Chinese restaurant. Whitey was a coffee drinker now, and put away at least six cups a day.

"I got my orders today," he said. "I've been assigned to an aircraft carrier, the "Coral Sea," with the Sixth Fleet. We'll be leaving from Norfolk next month."

Loretta was already used to hearing news like that, but she still dreaded it when it came. She knew she'd be moving again, this time to Virginia -- and Whitey would be gone for at least four or five months. She'd have plenty of company there in Norfolk. Navy wives are a strong sorority, and always have been, although they have always maintained the "officer," "enlisted," class system forced on them by the old Naval traditions.

"Loretta, I've got a chance to put in for `Limited Duty Officer.' It's a new program -- and if they accept me, I could be an ensign. We'd qualify for base housing and a good pay increase. What do you think?"

"Whitey, won't this "drying out" thing you've just been through hurt you? You've been in the program for six months. I know that they say you've got it all under control now, and I believe that you do too, but would they approve them if you put in the papers?"

"Commander DeLaval in personnel called me into his office and asked me to think about the LDO program, so I guess they've got some confidence in me. He knows my history. Hell, he had my personnel jacket on his desk when he talked to me. If they accept me, it would mean a good retirement check down the line, even though that's at least ten years away. Who knows? Maybe I could make it to Lieutenant Commander by then?"

Loretta reached across the table and grasped Whitey's hand, as she had once done in Jacksonville, eleven years before. He knew she was behind him, as she had always been during their marriage, and felt good about that.

"I'm so happy, Whitey. The Navy must feel that you can lick the alcoholism, and I knew you could. Now the Navy is showing you they've got confidence in you too! I'm so proud of you. Fill out the papers. You'll make a fine officer, I know it."

CHAPTER 52

The new year of 1992 had started off in a dull, drab way, like the last couple of years, Whitey thought. Nothing much new, a bit on the boring side. He hadn't been to a New Year's celebration in a long time. Hell, he wanted no part of the next-day hangovers, the headaches, wondering who he'd insulted or what women he'd made a play for the night before.

It may have been an article in a newspaper, or something in the American Legion magazine, perhaps a piece in the VFW's publication, he couldn't remember -- but Whitey heard of an organization called the Armed Guard Association, composed of Navy men and women who had served with that group in World War II. Curious, he wrote to the organization's headquarters, actually the home of one of its members, in Raleigh, North Carolina. Very quickly, an answering letter came back to Catskill, along with a copy of the group's newsletter, "The Pointer." Whitey was surprised to learn that the AG Association had just recently located their 10,000th member and added his name to the roster. A large number, perhaps, but not in comparison to the better than 144,000 men who had served in those dark days of the conflict. His interest was raised and dozens of thoughts began to flood his brain. Are any of my old shipmates still around? What have they been doing with themselves? Whatever happened to what's-his-name?

The Armed Guard Association was to have its 11th annual reunion, in New Orleans, in May, according to the "Pointer." Forty six years had gone down the drain since Whitey had been in New Orleans, just before he'd received his orders for Norfolk, and after that memorable Christmas with Loretta and her two daughters in Jacksonville.

He picked up the telephone and made travel reservations.

Whitey arrived at the airport on Wednesday afternoon and took a taxi to the Clarion Hotel, on Canal St., in New Orleans. Canal street passes close to the Superdome, on the banks of the Mississippi, and the Canal

Street ferry would take him across the river to Algiers, and the Naval Station, if he wanted to visit there. According to the schedule of events for the reunion, the group would be doing just that, Friday morning.

He registered for his room and had his bags taken there, then went to a table set up at the hotel's ballroom and registered for the reunion. He recognized no one at the table, or anywhere nearby, but the people were friendly. He rode the elevator to his room on the fifth floor, took a shower, changed clothes and went out into the city. Surprisingly, it was very much as he'd remembered it. The Superdome and the International Trade Mart, of course, were new to him, but he took another cab to the old French Quarter and wandered Bourbon, Royal and Charles streets. He and his shipmates had put down many a drink here, and enjoyed the good music, back in the days just after the war, when everyone was in a mood to celebrate, before returning home to their respective civilian lives.

Nostalgia was the order of the day and Whitey thought back to his many shipmates, some of whom he knew were dead, others who he hadn't seen in years, and probably would never see again.

When he'd satisfied himself in his wanderings about the old portion of the city, he returned to the hotel for what he thought would be a twenty-minute nap. He awoke with a start a bit past eight o'clock, then went to the hotel's restaurant and had a light supper, then walked the streets around the hotel until ten or eleven. Tired again, he came back to his hotel room and turned in for the night.

The hotel's hospitality room was open, and Whitey went there, right after having a big breakfast in the dining room of the hotel. He hadn't seen a familiar face yet, and was wondering if he'd made a mistake coming here. Was the money he'd spent wasted on a futile attempt to bring back some semblance of the "old days"?

An old man shuffled up to Whitey and stood there, staring intently at him. Whitey glanced at him, but no bells rang in his head, although there was something about the man that he just couldn't place.

"I never forget a face," said the old man. "Give me a minute and I'll place you -- shit yes, you're Chief Gunner's Mate Houston! Maybe you don't remember me -- Kennedy is the name."

Whitey looked carefully at him. Yes, the face was strangely familiar. Kennedy -- Kennedy, where had he heard that name? Then it came to him.

"Bainbridge, Maryland, 1951," exclaimed Whitey, smiling and shaking the man's hand. "You were my CO when I started training boots!"

"Damn right, Chief. You were a good man, as I recall. Had some trouble with the bottle, didn't you?"

"I'm sorry to say I did, Commander. Or, at least, that's what you were when I knew you. But I managed to get it together, finally. The Navy was good to me. What did you do after the war?"

"I retired in 1962 and went to the Citadel, in South Carolina, to teach mathematics. That's what my degree was in. Never did make it past commander, though. I retired once and for all about fourteen years ago. You know that I was a gunnery officer, but I was never an Armed Guard. I did my duty with the anti-sub bunch. I'm an "honorary" AG member, and proud to be one, Houston. How about you -- what road did you take?"

"I took the LDO route, Commander. Made a career of the Navy. Got out of active duty about twenty years ago, made it to Commander, same as you. I've been Chief of Police in Catskill, up in New York State, until two years ago. I heard somewhere about the Armed Guard Association and got myself down here -- used to be my old stamping grounds, at least until the end of the war."

"Houston -- damn, pardon me if I don't remember to call you Commander -- it's hard, after all these years. It's good to see you again. I'm glad that you've done well in the service, and out of it. I'm sure you'll be meeting some of your old shipmates here. Excuse me now, I've got to find my wife. She's probably looking for me -- thinks I'm getting senile, and maybe she's right."

With that, the old Commander shuffled off.

What a strange sensation the meeting caused in the pit of Whitey's stomach. It was as if the clock had turned backwards, leaving him in a time he thought he'd never experience again, but there were still surprises in store for him this day

"Whitey," called a fat bald-headed man from across the room.

"Whitey Houston, is that you?"

It was Tony DiNardi, who had been the best man at Whitey's wedding, back in 1946, and one of his friends aboard the Nantahala when he was on duty in the Mediterranean. Whitey hadn't seen Tony since 1950, but he knew DiNardi had made Warrant Officer, since they exchanged Christmas Cards and letters each year. He knew also that DiNardi had retired from the Navy a few years before he had, probably in 1968. Why they had never gotten together, he didn't know. Probably it was because DiNardi was back in Philadelphia and Whitey could find no excuse to go there. With the exception of a few pounds of weight around his middle and not much of his curly black hair left, the man still had not changed much.

DiNardi hurried across the room, reaching out and then putting his arms around Whitey. He moved fairly fast for a man who must be at least 72 or 73.

"Damn, Tony. I never expected to see you here."

"Why not, Whitey? I come to all the reunions -- but I've never seen you at one."

"Just joined the Association -- it was a last-minute thing, Tony. I wanted to get back to New Orleans, and this was a good excuse. Didn't we tie a few on when we were here?"

"My head aches just thinking about it. But things are different now. I don't touch a drop, Whitey. My stomach ulcer won't stand for it. Can't eat the spaghetti and meat balls either, Dammit."

"I'm sorry about Esther," said Whitey. Whitey had gotten the news of the death of DiNardi's wife in the previous Christmas letter that each man exchanged with the other.

DiNardi forced a smile.

"She was a good woman, Whitey. Stuck with me all through my Navy years, and way beyond. We had some tough times, believe me, but then I think you know that. And you know that I'm sorry about Loretta. God, Whitey, that woman was a beauty. Would you believe it, that was the only time in my life that anyone asked me to be their best man! When you sent me that Christmas card in 1960, it damn near ruined my holiday. You lost your mother, your mother-in-law and your wife, all the same year. You are a rugged sonofagun, Whitey. Don't know if I could have handled all that."

Whitey shook his head.

"Sometimes you do what you have to do. There's not much choice. Guess that's the story of my life, Tony."

"Are you taking the River Boat cruise tonight, Whitey?" asked Tony.

"Hell, why not? Sounds like it might be fun."

"I'll be there with my friend," said Tony, sheepishly. He motioned across the room at an attractive, short, grey-haired woman. "We've been going to a lot of places together -- feel sort of embarrassed about it, at my age, but what the hell, no reason to be lonely."

DiNardi shook hands, then walked off.

CHAPTER 53

The River Boat cruise was on the Natchez, a paddle-wheeler. The boat left its pier promptly at six, and a Cajun supper was served. Whitey enjoyed the spicy food and took a bit of a risk, drinking a bit more beer than he should have. He wasn't used to any kind of alcohol these days, and knew he was treading on dangerous ground.

A Dixie-Land band played aboard the boat, and as the darkness of night settled over the Mississippi, a full moon came out from behind the clouds, putting the boat's passengers in a mellow mood.

Whitey said hello to Tony DiNardi and his girl friend, but decided to steer clear of them, for fear of butting in. Commander Kennedy apparently had not signed on for the trip, understandable because the man was nearly eighty.

A group of seven men sat together, telling stories and laughing. Some of them had mixed drinks in their hands, and Whitey wandered over, nodded to them and sat down. He didn't want to intrude, but was feeling a little lonely, just a little drunk from all the beer he'd drunk. What the hell, he thought, might as well sit here and listen to the bullshit.

One of the men reached over to shake hands with Whitey.

"Haven't seen you at one of these reunions before," said the man. "Let me introduce myself. Chief Gunner's mate, retired, Rosario Silverio."

"Whitey Houston. Used to be a gunner myself, until the Navy made a mistake and let me into the LDO program. I just joined the AG organization, in fact I joined right here in New Orleans, at the hotel. I heard about the reunion and decided to come on down to the Crescent -- it's been a long time."

"Hold it," said another man, a tall, thin individual with a freckled face, bald head, and reddish eyebrows. "Whitey Houston -- hell, man, I was with you in London when the krauts sent those V-1's over and blew our barracks to hell. I'm Davey Jones -- they used to call me Jonesy!"

"I don't believe this," said another of the seven. "I'm Carlo Bitonte. We were on the Noordam together. That big luxury liner they were using to transport troops all over the friggin' Pacific."

"Will wonders never cease," murmured a third man. "I remember you, Houston. Back in Livorno -- I was head of the Shore Patrol one night -- I was a Lieutenant at the time -- and you and Jonesy got into a scrape with some tin can sailors in a bar. Did you really think I didn't know you'd cold-cocked that big son of a bitch with a chair? It was all I could do to keep from laughing. Do you remember me? Lieutenant O'Herlihy, from the SS Sam Morrison?"

"I'll be damned," said Whitey.

O'Herlihy continued. "I did thirty years in the Navy, Houston. Retired as a Captain. Somewhere or other I heard about you getting into the Limited Duty Officer program. They say you made Commander. Damn well done, I say."

"Camp Shelton," said Whitey. "Camp Shelton is where I met you, Silverio. You were a first class gunner's mate then. What a hole that place was."

"Damn right, Houston, but we cranked a lot of Armed Guard gunners out of there. Do you remember Commander Williford, the C.O. of Shelton? He got killed in an explosion off Okinawa in April of 1945. A kamikaze attack, it was."

"Yes, it isn't likely that I'd forget that," said Whitey. "My brother was an AG gunner aboard the SS Burgoyne during that same attack. His ship blew up, with him aboard. I lost my other brother in the Atlantic, a couple of days before the war ended in Europe. That year was one of the worst in my life."

"Sorry, Whitey," said Jonesy. "We've all got memories like that -- but what makes reunions like this worth it is the fact that we've all been through the same shit. There isn't anyone who can understand who hasn't been an Armed Guard gunner, and that's for sure."

The seven men talked, laughed and drank for the remainder of the paddle-wheel cruise. Whitey went to bed in his hotel room that night a very tired, but very happy man.

CHAPTER 54

Whitey snapped out of his reverie. It was akin to coming out of a dark movie theater, after a long and enjoyable show. The brilliant blazing sunlight would suddenly blind you, and as your senses adjusted themselves to the real world, there was a kind of emotional letdown. He was back in the world of 1992, and the feeling was not pleasant.

His father and mother, his brothers, Loretta, his shipmates down through the years -- nearly all of them dead and buried by now. He felt ancient and ready to be discarded by the modern world. As they used to say in the 60's, "What a bummer!"

When he'd returned from a Pacific cruise in the spring of 1960, Loretta told him of the doctor's discovery of her breast cancer. It was a heart-breaking year. Loretta's cancer was well-advanced -- the medics weren't catching it then as they are now, and Loretta was gone before Christmas.

Whitey's son Jack entered Annapolis in the fall of that year. Jack followed his father's footsteps and made a career of the Navy, becoming a Navy pilot five years later.

Both Loretta's mother and Mrs. Houston passed away the same year, both from heart attacks and both in the spring. Poor Loretta was hit from all sides with bad news. But young Jack Houston was a tough kid. He'd cried at the funerals -- all three of them, but seemed to come out of it all with the characteristic toughness that his mother and grandmother had both displayed.

Whitey did not fare as well as his son and had come close to reverting to his old drinking habits. It was his son Jack who set the example for his father, and sustained him through that terrible and painful period of his life.

Whitey "hung it up" with his beloved Navy in 1972, after thirty years. He was proud to have moved up to full commander, an unusual accomplishment for a "mustang" who'd never attended college a day in his life.

His wartime record and distinguished naval service had helped him become the Chief of Police in Catskill, in 1975. He'd moved back there right after retiring, and was living in his parents' old house. Phil Harrison was retired now, and had moved to Florida with his wife Ruthie.

Whitey's final retirement was from the Catskill police department, in 1990.

The Armed Guard Reunion in New Orleans in May had been a wonderful experience for Whitey. A new world had opened up -- a world of his former shipmates, and other AG men who had been through much the same experiences as himself. These were people he could talk with, people who understood him. Many of them had made careers of the Navy, and it is true that career military people have a different outlook on life than people who have never had that adventure.

He thought about his 67 years and wondered idly if he'd contributed anything worthwhile to his country. Yes, it was true that he and many of his shipmates had fought off enemy attackers, helping their merchant vessels get through to port with the essential tools of war. And they had survived sinkings, fires and explosions, but that was all a matter of survival. Nothing heroic or noble in that.

Perhaps he'd inspired some of those boots he'd helped train, back in Bainbridge in 1951 and 1952. He was proud of his young sailors' achievements, and occasionally heard from one or two of them. Some had gone on to distinguish themselves in the Navy. Didn't one particular recruit from Iowa go right to the Naval Academy, immediately after finishing his boot training? Of course. He reflected on how many others might have decided to "sign over" after their first hitch and make a career of it.

One thing for damn sure -- if they had stayed in the Navy, and eventually gotten married, they'd had to have had strong and understanding wives. He'd seen the service sink many a couple's marriage. His own Loretta should have gotten a medal, he mused, putting up with him and still managing to raise three kids, almost singlehandedly.

At the moment, he was depressed, but thought -- what the hell, he had plenty of people who cared about him. His stepdaughters, Donna and Karen, were both married. Donna and her husband were in San Diego, California and had a son. Karen and her husband had never left Florida, and had twins, a boy and a girl. Whitey loved those three grand kids, and sometimes flew south, or to the west coast, for a short visit. Occasionally they'd come to Catskill. He had plenty of room in the old Houston house.

Although he'd never admit it, Whitey was proudest of all of his son Jack. Jack had turned out to be one of Catskill's most respected adopted native sons, although he had been born in Florida. Jack Houston was a Vice-Admiral these days, the flag officer of the Navy's Sixth Fleet in the Mediterranean, and the only flag officer in history to have once been an astronaut, although his time in that group was an abbreviated one. He'd only been involved in the training of other astronauts, and had never actually been in space.

Unfortunately, Whitey could not claim any grandchild from Jack. The Navy had been a demanding profession, and Jack and his wife Miko had been divorced only a few years after they first married. They had met in Yokosuka, Japan, when Jack's carrier was there. Jack never tied the knot again. Miko had moved to San Francisco and remarried.

Whitey Houston -- few people in the town of Catskill called him that. He'd been addressed as Chief Houston in his years as the town Chief of Police and they still called him Chief.

How damn ironic, he thought. Of all his brothers, he was the one everyone thought was destined for jail or a bad end. Wild, undisciplined, irresponsible, a constant problem to his parents and to the local police.

What had changed the course of his life? Thinking back, he had to give credit to his brother Jack Houston. It wasn't anything his brother had done -- although he knew that Jack had done everything in his power to steer him onto the straight and narrow, and failed. But it was Whitey's unadmitted and undeterred admiration for his older brother, his pain at Jack's terrible death and his anger at those people, the Nazi war machine, that had caused it.

He wasn't angry with the people of Catskill, even though they'd never bothered to replace the plaque that had been placed by the flag pole in the town square, honoring Jack Houston. It disappeared sometime in the 60's, during the anti-Vietnam war riots and commotion. The same people, or at least the children of those people, whose country had been saved by the likes of Whitey and his brothers, rioted and demonstrated against the military.

It's human nature for people to forget, and Whitey understood. But he would not forget. Tomorrow morning he'd go over to the Mayor's office and see if the town would think about putting up a new plaque. Hell, he thought, after fifty years, the bastards owe Jack at least that much. And it will be done, even if I have to pay for it myself.

THE END

───────────────

They were the stepchildren of the Navy -- the "other Navy" -- all but unknown today. But they helped their shipmates, the merchant marine, deliver the troops, guns and essential goods of war, wherever they were needed, throughout the world. They were the gunners, boatswains, coxswains, signalmen, medics and radiomen of the Naval Armed Guard.

They served aboard more than 6000 merchant vessels and 1810 of them gave their lives in the line of duty.

They did it because it had to be done and there was no one else to do it.

"The boys did not get the carriers or battleships of their dreams, but they got something else from their time in the Armed Guard. They learned about the world and the people in it. They rode the subways of New York, transitted the Canal, saw the villages of the middle east, and the towns and cities of Brazil, Australia and other far-flung places. They grew up and became better men while the Navy was fulfilling its long-standing promise, `Join the Navy and See the World.'"

                                        - Lieutenant Commander Norman Alston - AG

"They Aimed To Deliver" is a historical novel that tells the story of the Houston brothers -- a merchant mariner, a marine, and three Armed Guard sailors, whose lives spanned the years of World War II. Their experiences are a chronicle of the high and low points of America's battle with the forces of Imperial Japan and Nazi Germany.

To order extra copies of this book, send $15 and your mailing address to:

TATD
P.O. Box 4194
Cary, N.C. 27519-4194

Your book(s) will be shipped to you within ten days, postage paid.